UNTHOLOGY 4

2013

UNTHANK
BOOKS

First published in 2013
By Unthank Books
www.unthankbooks.com

Printed in England by Lightning Source, Milton Keynes

All Rights Reserved

A CIP record for this book is available from the British Library

Any resemblance to persons fictional or real who are living, dead or
undead is purely coincidental.

ISBN 978-0-9572897-4-1

Edited by Robin Jones and Ashley Stokes

Cover image © Nicolas Ruston
Design & typeset by Tommy Collin

Contents
UNTHOLOGY 4

INTRODUCTION

The Editors

Ismism

Tickboxexotica. Decontentization. Flashism. Tedium Worship. Carver-Palaverism. Flock-of-Seagulls Haircut-Realism. Insider-Artism. Trustafarian Minimalism. Kneejerk Liberalism. Coffee-Table Fascism. Retro-Radicalism. PoemEnvy. Reflex-Surrealism. Surveyism. *The Loss-Adjuster of Nagorno-Karabakh.* Commissarism. Arbiterization. Nabob Statism. Market-Defeatism. Spleen-rejectionism. Rearguardism. Beeism. TemplateFetishization. AntiHighConceptism. The Canadian slipstream fiction-journals *Goosestep Meringue Underpass, Squamous Baboon* and *Sulphuric Phlox Aberration.* Crash-Hackery. CarterGymkhanaism. Victim-Grubbery. KnobwithPhDism. SoftTargetization. Identity-Parade Showmanship. Jismism. LuxuryRetailerAbroadism. *The Pâtissier of Phnom Penh.* Donkeyworkism. MunchkinPromoterism. AmWritingism. BorderlineNonceism/OutrightNonceism. Woodwindyism. BasqueSeparatistPoetwithGovernmentGrantism. Countism. ShellfishAnthropomorphism. YAFantasyTrilogyKindleism. Death-Fellationism. Chin-Lickery. ObligatoryElvisism. PrizeWinnerCapitulationism. SameThemeTrapism. TargetGroupHedging. Campus Moronism. RabbitWarrenHawHawism. The machinations of the talentless one-hundred-and-twelve-year-old-man (Cadaver Localism, or GibberingCorpseRegionalism). IntestinalJanusism. List-Death. DownBraining. AntiProfanity. AntiEmotionalism. UnderMilkFloatism. Zeroism. Obviousism. Category Mining.

Introduction

The experimental poetry journals *Panda Glands* and *Zygotes of Nimoy*. SameOldFaceism. SpambotPRism. Git-Lit. Gitism. Workshyism. Idiotwithmoneyism. The Neverhadajobist Movement. HorizontalListEntryism. ChildEyeInfantilizationism. ShortStoryPackagedasNovelAgendaization. PatOnBackHandInPocketism. TranslationGimpery. RepetitionFetishizationism. Cliqueism. LeprechaunGatekeeperism. The Prosaic Banner Phenomena. NowBlindness. CircusDefaultism. AntiUsism. Can'tSayItOutLoudism.

Unthology: Four and Against.

A REAL T.O.A.

Rodge Glass

Your eyes have been closed so long that the light seems artificial now, surely too bright to be real. Your eyelids are cling film. Your armpits are furnaces; your fingers lit matches, waiting to burn out. This climate, it's a killer. You've seen what it can do.

As you're lying on the beach, flickering, the light whipping of the wind sounds like a storm in your eardrums. The sky is being squeezed from either side and giant unseen hands are pressing towards each other as the earthquakes of the last few months rip in – to her in the water, to you on the land. This feels like one long shaking. It feels like it'll never stop, and the fact you're both still here, it's what Rosie's Uncle Jaro would call a real T.O.A. *Sometimes,* his last phone message said, *it's worth congratulating yourself for going another whole day without somersaulting off a bridge.* The man is a suicide-in-waiting. You've told Rosie to stop taking his calls. Meanwhile, someone's walking a dog further up the beach. It keeps barking and the volume is going north, and as the barking turns to a howling you think that really, dogs are noisier than they need to be. What is it they're so desperate to communicate? Christ, all they do is eat, shit, sleep and stay loyal. And none of that is anything to shout about.

The sun seems to be getting brighter. It's a cheap lamp shining in your eyes, a high street changing room, and the last thing you want to do is face the light. Your limbs are lead weights fixed in position, and the more you hide the more the outside world threatens to burst through. You're behind bars here, waiting for questioning. Hold on: if this is prison then why is there sand in your cell? The view isn't your typical prison view either. It's the inside of your eyelids, a vague, warm, spiralling kaleidoscope. You strain to shut out the pressure. Your mind is in the sky now, and you're thinking that maybe your skull is an open prison – one of those where you can kid yourself that you're free, and nothing needs to change. You press your fingers into your temples. Then squeeze.

In the heat, confusion. You wonder if interrogators will visit you in prison, and if they do, what they'll say your crimes are. Negligence, perhaps. What other charge could there be? You see this sort of thing all the time in the glossies Rosie leaves by the bath, whispering, *Pick Me Up*. Sometimes guys don't even know they're in trouble until it's too late – they feel like Superman but find out in the pages of *Real Lives* that they're Boyfriends from Hell – and ignorance is no excuse. For the girls in the glossies, expectations are clear. And there's no disciplinary process. There are no written warnings. *He couldn't give,* says Tracey from Scarborough – *and I couldn't give any more. I deserved better.* Ten thousand regular readers break into applause while you tense your toes, bringing them up into a tight ball. Your stretch out your bird legs and spread your claws into the sand below. The ground trembles. Where's Rosie? You look around. Sense something. The sun is pushing the sky onto your chest again, heavier this time, more insistent. Like it's getting impatient for change. Maybe Jaro is right, maybe just still *being* here is a victory. You should get yourself to a bar. Take a table with a sea view. Order champagne. *What's the occasion Sir?* the barman will ask. And you'll say: *I'm not in pieces on the rocks. It's a real Triumph Over Adversity.*

Only there's no barman, no bubbly, and you feel like the only person in New Zealand. That's become a regular sensation recently but, like the heaviness, it's probably an illusion so why think of it? Better to concentrate on the known. Do as you're told and follow instructions. Keep calm and prove you can stay that way: that's what's required. So you take the iPod out of the bag, scroll

[4]

through the options, press Play and turn up the volume, just like you promised. There's an empty sound, a light buzzing, then noise. The voice in your head is a cool burr – a patient, timelessness that sounds like home and shuts out everywhere else. This is what the Loch back home would say if it could talk. You focus on the voice. The Loch is speaking. Its waves leak through your headphones, the branches of the trees on its banks wrap their arms around you. The Loch introduces itself as Doctor Alistair MacLeod and whispers: *THIS IS QUICK RELAXATION.*

Which you could do with.

As the instructions begin you can smell the Highlands, cold and damp and salty on your tongue, like sweat. It's so strong you think you must be asleep. But then the smell is gone, whisked away by the breeze. You open your eyes, strain to adjust, see the near-empty beach and wonder: what are you both doing here? And how can you get away? You look down the sand towards the bars and wonder if that's the way home. Sure, the walk would take months, maybe years. You'd have to buy a boat or make friends with a sailor. But at least you'd be moving; there'd be a job to do. *And now I want you to tense your neck,* says the Loch. *Push your chin down towards your chest, as far as you can. Feel that tension. Feel it. Now let it go.* The voice is everything, and then nothing, because there she is. You see just the back of her, white foam spilling out from the corners of the patterned blue hugging her legs, running over her like hands. She's the size of your thumb now, and going outwards.

Rosie's wearing the swimsuit she bought for the last holiday, and you can't look at it without thinking about the things you haven't done since. Though you swore to never let time steal by again, unmarked by movement, there were always reasons why you couldn't follow up on the Mexico trip. Good ones. There were other people's weddings. Other people's babies. There was always work, and Christmas seemed to come along every few months. But now work is a hunger that's eaten everything, there's only more of it when you get home, and you can't remember what getting up in the morning is supposed to be for. Three summers ago Rosie said, *We're getting thinner*, and you promised to change – but the illness got comfy in your shared bed, you served it tea, fed the thing till it was fat. No amount of sun can make up for that now. This brightness reminds her there hasn't been more of it, and to her you'll always be the boy who couldn't grow up in time. As you lie on New Zealand sand, the last few years seem heavy and hollow. But not everything does. Even now, when you watch her, all you see is sunshine. You sit up. Focus. You might not be able to look at her much longer.

Rosie's got the fingers of both hands splayed, running them through the water as she skips further into the Coral Sea. You follow her movement. If she keeps going like that she'll eventually hit the South Pacific, then a while later, New Zealand. You wonder if that's what she wants – and if it is, whether you should wade in to stop it. Carry her back to shore. Pick her up and put her over your shoulder while she screams and tells you to let her go. To stop this thought growing you close your eyes again and sink back into the sand. You realise that if she looks to shore, all Rosie will be able to see is you lying down. Carrying on as if she wasn't there, like you always do. For a moment she might forget what colour your eyes are. A shiver might dance down her spine, she'll remember, and then wonder why she's been paralysed for so long. What next? She'll play in the sea a while. The water is warm. She doesn't swim enough. Rosie will collapse back into the blue, clench her fists, then let go.

The Loch takes a breath.

Even with your eyes closed, everything's clear.

Rosie's legs and arms are white like the walls of your living room. Her eyes are green like your front door. And away from home, she tans on her shoulders, burns on her forearms and blonde streaks are borne into the darkness of her hair. You can't remember anything before these splashes of colour, the freckles on her back, and don't want to think about life after them. Life which is coming, whether you want it or not. Meanwhile the Loch in your ears says: *Now tense the muscles in your arms – tense them, tense them, make them as tense as you can. Wait…wait…and now relax. Feel the tension seeping out of you, out, out, into the atmosphere. Imagine seeing tension flying away into the sky. Up into the clouds and disappearing. See? Doesn't that feel good?*

You think about the whole last year and more, just wriggling free that easily. About reversing time by simply tensing your muscles and releasing – breathing heat into cold lungs, sucking weakness from your marrow, your mind. You think about more than the physical. About unsaying all your spoken mistakes and everyone else's too. Mending friendships lost through distance and sensible decision-making. Sliding bank accounts from red into black while you're at it. This idea makes you want to laugh a long, empty laugh, but you're so deep now, below the surface of the beach, the ground, so close to the centre of the earth that you have to think about some stranger laughing instead – but who? The kind of man she'll notice, once she's free. Or maybe the kind she's noticed already. In that case, this is a different story.

Meanwhile she's swimming, and you promised to join her. She could be stalling, hoping you'll run right in there and join her. Who knows, it could be worth going in. But the water here stings the cuts on your arms, the backs of your legs, even all over your feet, and in this land of cool golden bodies and endless heat the cuts seem to be resisting the healing instinct: so you won't be in the water any time soon. Nothing heals fast enough here. It makes you heavy, but maybe these demons are imaginary. Maybe there's more time to heal after all. *And now I want you to clench your fists* says the cool Loch, blowing out a thousand years of peaceful nothingness. *Clench them tight, tight, tighter…take all of your tension and channel it into your fists.* You feel energy rushing at your knuckles.

Next, the Loch instructs you to unlock your fingertips, your shoulders, your thighs. You've gotten to know it well in the last few weeks, the Play Count says you've listened to Doctor Alistair MacLeod's 'Instructions for Calm' thirty-three times since leaving Inverness, so you know Quick Relaxation is nearly over for today. It continues playing, but someone's fading the volume out, slowly, slowly. *Free yourself*, says the Doctor, so quiet it feels like you must be imagining him. *There's no need to hold yourself back. It's the holding that's the problem.* His voice muted now, and this makes you think about opening your eyes. About rubbing your back into the sand like a bear snuggling into the spine of a tree, teasing out the itch. All you really want to do is tease out the itch. If you explain that to Rosie, surely she'll understand. You sit up and open your eyes.

It takes a few seconds to adjust to this new world. You scan the yellow. You can't see her there. She's not in the water either. You scan the coastline, too fast to register anything. You're certain she's gone, and if that's what she wants then that's the way it should be. You were raised well, you won't resist. And you don't blame her for growing tired. God knows you're tired too. Everyone is tired or bored or starting over. But what if that's not it – what if she's drowned? What are you gonna do if she's drowned? You'd drive your plane into the ground. You'd somersault off that bridge. A hot rush fills your head as you see it. But just then, as you see the land rushing closer from mid-air, a hand appears out of the water, which turns into an arm, which turns into a woman. She's wet and shaking her head back and forth. You've seen these movements on beaches far from here. You feel the distance. The Loch whispers, *And now you should feel totally...completely...relaxed.*

Then it stops.

Rosie swims further away once more; it feels like she's always turning to go further away, and meanwhile you're transported to a dark room on the other side of the planet. It's after the unravelling. Your curtains are drawn during the day. You think about trying to make a new room into a home while your new Hungarian flat-mate cooks a broth whose smell creeps under the doors and hugs the walls. You think about what is yours, what is hers, what you'd throw away if there was no one around to remind you what's sensible and how really *you might as well think of the future.* Without even leaving the beach, you're there, in that future. Damp stains the corners of the bedroom. It's dusty. The last tenant left behind boxes labelled FRAGILE and that's enough to make you want to take a swan dive. But you can choose the music and come home any time. You can leave the window open, set the shower to maximum heat and there'll be no glossies in the bathroom.

The last one's a killer.

Today she might come back. But the water has woken her and now she feels like she's been asleep for years. The water talks, and whispers that you're the one who's been keeping her eyes shut, holding her eyelids together all this time, hoping she wouldn't realise what else could be hers. And maybe you have been doing that. You didn't sanction it, didn't sign anything, but maybe you did.

Either way, this is happening. It's in the way she dives and dances in the water like a dolphin, splashing around in the blue. It's so obvious; you can't believe you didn't see it before. You scroll the iPod to your current favourite album, hit Play and the first thing the machine breathes out is the words, *Leaving is easy if you've got someplace you need to be.* You don't know what you'd do without these songs. They're medicine. And the dose is almost enough to cancel out what's about to be lost. Sitting up, hands locked together between your knees, you look over towards the bars and see what's coming:

1) *Who you'd have to tell.* You think about how you'd get the words out and what friends and family would say back. You'd have to admit you thought you were two successful magicians welded together at the hip and head, and how it's turned out you're just another romantic who believed in magic.

2) *Sleeping alone.* You think about whether you'd just crack and end up one morning in Uruguay, nails painted blue, dancing the tango, solo, right there in bed. Deep in the nightmare, kicking the covers to the hostel floor while the Italian couple in the bunk opposite go for it one more time.

3) *Someone else.* You think about meeting someone new with eyes of a different colour who thinks you smell of fresh bread in the bakery and taste of summer strawberries and feel like a radiator in the night. Who locks into you and fits, spies you standing naked in the light and wants to look for longer. Reaches into your guts and draws out something hot and healthy you didn't even know was there.

You can see all this but can't feel it. You wonder how long it will take before you can feel again.

You could do with a fucking beer.

Out here, Rosie's been phoning home a lot, talking to her mum for hours, and calling Jennifer, and calling Uncle Jaro. This morning Jaro said that in French they call what the two of you have been through is called a *Serie Noire.* You told her to pass a message back – that in English they call the same thing a Triumph Over fucking Adversity. But in order to triumph over something, you have to survive it first, right? Yeah, it's coming apart, all this. But maybe you'll talk it out. In the time it takes for this thought to crystallize, it's followed by another. The headache gets hotter, the ball in your brain doubles and your temples throb. Your head is a bonfire and once more the sky is squeezed. Where you come from, they call this guilt. You're making contingencies when you should be making one last pitch. You might as well say *Thanks for your interest,* shake hands and make excuses right now. Split the beach bag and head in different directions. Should you? It's more dignified than what's coming.

Rosie returns to land quicker than expected – she was so far out, she must have flown back. But already she's standing above you, drying her hair, and she can't help smiling. She says, *I wish I could do that every day.* You tell her, *There's no reason why you can't* and touch her leg. She answers, *Tell that to my schedule,* then wraps the shawl around her hips, slides her feet into sandals and withdraws. Despite everything, both of you will delay going back to the apartment. Back there, the inevitable is obvious. You watch her for a moment, and she watches you watching. She wonders if you know. And she lets it go, because for now, nothing can be done.

Such things cannot be executed on holiday. All you can do is take deep breaths and continue. Try not to fight. Sleep without touching. The days are long, and you're here for the next ten days. At home, you can split sensibly down the middle. Once the jet lag has worn off and the cost of everything can be counted. But for now you need to hold your breath and stand behind each other in case one of you falls. That's what love is, right? And love is all you can call it. Meanwhile, New Zealand is nothing. You can't see it. You just have to close your eyes until it goes away. So you stand, brush the sand from your chest, hold out a hand and wonder if she'll accept. *Try me a little longer,* you say. Rosie gives a kind of smile, takes the offered hand and answers, *Come on, I'm thirsty. Let's go and get a drink.*

Her wings spread out and flap.

The gust of wind is so strong it knocks you from your feet.

Your muscles tense. Then relax.

TREASURES OF HEAVEN

Carys Bray

The first time you met, he reminded you of the strapping, Anglo-Saxon Jesus from the religious paintings in your parents' house. He was searching for Middle-Eastern journals in the university library and while you helped him, he told you about his work with a writers' group in Palestine. You considered bringing up his resemblance to Aryan-Jesus, but couldn't think of a sane way to say it. Instead, you mentioned your writing. He ignored your nervous laugh. He asked questions and made suggestions about where to send stories. Later, he came back to the library with a signed copy of his novel.

'There you are,' he said. 'Keep writing, and don't be shy about it.'

You enjoyed the novel. Part of the enjoyment came from imagining him write it, especially the sex that was both tender and enthusiastically executed. You were curious about which depictions belonged to him and which were invented. Each time he returned to the library, you thought about the line between experience and fiction and wondered whether he had hidden little pieces of himself in the pages of his novel.

You met unexpectedly at the book fair this afternoon. He told you about his summer trip to Palestine and you told him about your first publication. When he gave you a swift hug, you stood very still, surprised at the effectiveness with which you have unremembered touch.

'We should have a drink to celebrate.'

'I'd love to, but I've got a train to catch.'

'Go on, just a quick one,' he said.

The pub is dark and cavernous, stuffed with oak furniture and enclosed by red, flocked walls. London is gusting with heat. It's cooler indoors, but the air is still warm, blaring and pulsing with guitar chords and drums from a nearby speaker.

The faces of saints are luminous, stoked with patience and goodness - he has such a face. He is the only person in the pub who exists in soft focus. It's as if his edges have been sanded to gentleness. You watch as he talks to one of the bar staff. He speaks with his mouth and his hands, and when his fingers fan, the spaces between them flash like smiles. You can see his wedding band. It's chunky and polished, like a tiny halo. You suppose he loves his wife, which adds another bar to the tally of his goodness.

He smiles as he carries the drinks to the table.

'So you came on the train. This morning?'

He hands you a glass of wine.

'Yes, I came early so I could go to the British Museum.'

'Ah, it's wonderful. Isn't the roof incredible? What's your favourite thing? The mummies are mine. Did you like them?'

'I didn't get that far. I went to Treasures of Heaven, the new exhibit - saints and relics.'

'Ah. Are you Catholic?'

'No. No, I'm not.'

'Religious?'

You shake your head.

'Me neither. Not got much time for any of it, to be honest. So what was the appeal of Treasures of Heaven?'

'I'm not sure.'

'Go on,' he says. 'There's a story there. Otherwise you'd have looked at the mummies like the rest of us. I bet it was just you and a load of old blokes - retired priests, monks and a few religious nutters.'

'There *were* a lot of old blokes,' you concede. 'It was interesting. I wanted to see it because, well, my parents - they're very religious.'

[14]

'Oh God, I'm embarrassed now. Sorry.'

His apologetic hand brushes your arm. You make a don't-worry-about-it gesture, slide your arm under the table, out of the way, and take another swallow of wine.

'So, did you enjoy it?'

'It was...' you pause in search of the right words. 'It was gruesome, but magical. There were so many incredible stories. Did you know St. Margaret was swallowed by a dragon, but she made the sign of the cross and burst through its belly button, like a superhero?'

You reach under the table for your bag. You dig around for a moment, push past your purse, your phone and a pair of flip-flops and pull out a notebook that's teeming with unfamiliar, consonant-heavy words like *triptych*. You aren't sure whether you will do anything with these words; they inhabit an area of thinking which you deliberately cordon off.

'Ah-ha. You made notes. You're going to write about it.'

'I might.'

'You should.'

'There were so many beautiful things – all these lovely relics, but at the heart of each was a piece of a dead person. There was this icon, The Man of Sorrows. It was like a grisly advent calendar: two hundred little drawers containing two hundred tiny pieces of dead saints. Even though I knew what was inside, I still wanted to unlock the glass case and open the little drawers.'

'Hiding the ugly truth inside something beautiful, that's all they're doing,' he says, and he rests his hand on your arm again, in a friendly, emphasising way. His fingers are gentle and warm, partitioned by fine knuckle-creases. He has short nails and blunt finger-tips. It's been a long time since a man has touched your bare skin, and you are surprised to realise that you would like to touch him back. 'Things turned out pretty badly for the saints, didn't they?' he continues. 'God, just imagine what's in store for sinners!' His smile classifies sin as funny, abstract, and old-fashioned. 'You're a lapsed follower, right? I suppose that makes you a sinner!'

'I suppose it does.'

'Did you have to do the whole confession thing?'

A long glug of wine buys you some time to formulate a reply.

*

There was no anonymity in the confessional and there was nothing mystical or priestly about the ecclesiastical authority. He was your friend's dad, in a Top Man suit. His name was Steve, but you had to call him Bishop. He ushered you into his office during Sunday school. He sat on a swivel chair, behind a big desk and asked a list of set questions. You sat opposite, on a brown, plastic seat. You were twelve, drowning in a Laura Ashley dress and a pair of your mother's flesh coloured tights, for modesty.

'Do you have a testimony of *The Book of Mormon*?' he asked.

It was an easy question. You knew the right answer was yes. But there were other, harder questions.

'Are you chaste?'

'Chased?'

'Do you live the Law of Chastity?'

You knew the Law of Chastity was about sex. You weren't familiar with the particulars, but you hadn't kissed anyone, hadn't even held a boy's hand. At that stage, sex was more than you could imagine, so you definitely lived the Law of Chastity. Definitely.

'Yes,' you said.

'And can you explain what that means?'

He propped his clasped hands on the desk where they rested like a stack of hairy sausages and he gave you a hard stare. Your parents believed he had the spirit of discernment, that he could see right into your soul. You looked away and he interpreted your hesitation as ignorance.

'Let's run through it,' he said. 'The first things we think of when we talk about chastity are adultery and fornication. You're a bit young for them! More importantly, for now, we're talking about sins like petting and necking.' He pulled a pamphlet out of a drawer in his desk while you tried to imagine actions for the unfamiliar words. 'And sexual stimulation of the self, masturbation,' he added as he opened up the pamphlet.

You remembered years ago, balancing your violin case against your groin as you buttoned up your coat. It was nice. You did it again, after your coat was buttoned, and your mother said, 'Stop it. That's dirty.'

One night when you couldn't sleep you accidentally discovered if you rubbed just there, you could make yourself pop like a rocket. You wondered if you'd made a unique discovery, or if other people could do it too. Later on, when you were a bit older, lads at school joked about having a tug, being wankers, tossers, and you wondered if there was another word, a nicer one, for girls, one that described the thing you could do. You looked up wanker in the dictionary: *N, someone who masturbates; a worthless, contemptible person.* You'd never seen the word *masturbate* before. Your parents never mentioned it. They didn't say it was a sin when they explained about the sacred powers of procreation and never letting anyone except your future husband touch, or see, the parts of you a one-piece swimsuit should cover.

You tried not to worry about what the Bishop had just said. Instead, you concentrated on the front of his pamphlet. *Love vs. Lust.* It sounded like a football league fixture.

'Masturbation is a damnable transgression,' he read. 'It is the gateway to the acts of fornication and adultery.' He put the pamphlet down for a moment and gave you a long, penetrating stare. 'Have you been engaging in self-stimulation?'

You quite liked yourself up until that moment. You thought you were a good girl and you imagined you had a fine shot at getting a pretty high score in the test of life. You believed in God, in the certainty of The Right and in the easiness of always choosing it.

'I didn't know it was wrong,' you said, staring down at the meaty heap of his fingers.

'How did you find out about it?' he asked. 'Did someone tell you? Did you read about it in a magazine?'

You tried to put your accidental wickedness into language, but you didn't own the words to answer.

'Do you understand repentance? In order to repent, you must forsake the sin. That means you must *never* do it again.' He reached down into his briefcase and pulled out his scriptures. He opened his Doctrine and Covenants and read; 'Go your ways and sin no more; but unto that soul who sinneth shall the former sins return.'

He closed his scriptures and patted them. 'You can be forgiven, but if you sin again, you'll go back to the start and you'll have to repent of every sin again. It's best to nip this in the bud, before it gets more serious. You do know that sexual sin is next to murder in seriousness?'

You nodded, crossed your legs and tried to resist the impulse to adjust your mother's baggy tights.

'You need to tell your parents about this,' he said.

'Oh, I really can't.' You'd have begged, if you hadn't been so certain that pleading would take the lid off your upset and expose you as a great big cry baby.

'It's part of the repentance process,' he replied, with a sad smile and a shrug, making it clear that you couldn't possibly argue with God's requirements.

He made small talk for a minute or two, asked about your violin playing and advised you to only listen to worthy music. You didn't ask for clarification; you loved all kinds of music and didn't want the responsibility of knowing what was unworthy. Finally, he stood and held out a damp, fleshy hand for you to shake. 'Go thy way and sin no more,' he said.

You wanted forgiveness, and you realised it could only be purchased by wading through shame, so you told your parents straight after church. Telling them was more frightening than playing Vivaldi's Concerto in A Minor in a school assembly.

'Oh dear, nice girls don't do that,' your mother said.

You opened your mouth to reply, but nothing came out.

'Never ruin an apology with an excuse,' she advised.

Your dad coughed and muttered something you didn't quite catch. They addressed you as if you were standing next to them, but only your body was there. The *you* part, the bit inside, had collapsed in a deep cringe. You could feel it hiding in a knot near your sternum, curled up like a crustacean.

*

'We had these things called Bishop's interviews. They involved confessing, but it wasn't like Catholic confession. No *Hail Marys.*

No consecrated relics or indulgences.'

'I'm sure Chaucer would be pleased to hear it,' he says.

You smile at each other and he nods, indicating he would like to hear more, but you ignore his cue.

'There were books that predated Chaucer at the exhibition. There were even a few from the eleven hundreds. They were gorgeous. They had really bright illustrations and the writing – it was beautiful.'

'More books?' he says. 'You're surrounded by them every day.'

'But these were special. They had these wooden board covers and the paper was made out of parchment. I couldn't help but wonder where they'd been during the last nine hundred years and how many people had read them. And it was strange to think that all those people – the people who made the books and the people who read them - are dead, but the books are still alive. It made me want to pick them up and turn their pages. But I couldn't, they were in display cases.'

'Yeah, and you know why they were in display cases? To stop people like you from illicit book-touching.'

'It would have been nice to touch them. I bet you'd have thought so too.'

'It's always nice to touch things,' he says.

You probably shouldn't notice the way the skin at the top of his nose concertinas when he smiles. You shouldn't appreciate the deep, friendly creases that bracket his mouth like chevrons. And you certainly shouldn't wonder if pressing your lips to his might enable you to siphon some of his goodness.

'It's hot today, isn't it?'

He nods agreement while you unpeel the backs of your legs from the wooden chair and try to think of something to say.

'It's like with writing,' he says. 'Some things can be researched, but others have to be felt and touched. I couldn't have written about Palestine if I hadn't actually been there. I'd have got things wrong. South of the West Bank, there are places where the sand is almost red, not yellow, and it tastes like bricks. I know, I know - I've never eaten bricks. But it's dusty sand, not the grainy kind you get at the seaside. And if you open your mouth, little particles drift in and stick to your teeth. If I'd never been there, never touched it myself, I wouldn't know.'

*

It was the idea of *never* that made abstinence so difficult.

'Is it something I can do after I'm married?' you asked the Bishop.

'No! Rousing sexual feelings before marriage is wrong, but even after marriage you must exercise self-control.'

There was a small vase of flowers on the windowsill in his office - early daffodils and a couple of tulips. He reached across and pulled out a tulip, dripping water on the desk.

'Do you like flowers?'

'Yes.'

'Watch this,' he said as he pinched a red petal and rubbed it between thumb and index finger. He moved onto the next petal, and the next - rub, rub, rub. 'Do you want it, now?' He held the tulip out. The head drooped and the petals were bruised where he'd crushed them.

'Thank you.' You stretched forward to receive it, but he frowned and shook his head until you changed your mind. 'Sorry. I mean no. No, I don't want it.'

'That's right,' he said. 'Who'd want it now? Girls are like flowers.' He put the tulip back in the vase where it looked grubby and injured. 'Good men don't want girls who've been... handled.'

He offered plenty more advice in subsequent interviews. Never touch yourself except when you go to the toilet. Avoid being alone. Always keep a copy of *The Book of Mormon* nearby. Think of lying in a bathtub of worms and eating several of them whenever you sin. When tempted, skip a meal or two; it will divert physical energy into something more productive.

You decided lunch was the best meal to miss. Your mother reminded you not to forget your sandwiches as she left for work in the mornings. You put them in your blazer pocket and threw them in a bin on your way to school. You weren't sure what productive thing your physical energy was being diverted to, especially after you made the decision to miss breakfast as well. Your stomach spent any spare energy making thundering demands for food, but people said you looked good. Bones buoyed your wrists, your clavicles emerged like a pair of tildes and your stomach shrivelled into a hollow, cramping pocket. You enjoyed the pain - it confirmed that you were loathsome on the inside. You didn't need a portrait in the attic, you were unremittingly conscious of your inner ugliness.

'I don't like Bishop's interviews,' you told your mother.

'What doesn't kill us makes us stronger,' she said.

Finally, you forsook your sin.

'That's good news,' the Bishop said. 'But repentance is more than saying sorry. If you haven't suffered, you haven't repented. When you've repented properly, the Lord will remember your sins no more.'

'But how will I know when I've repented enough? How will I know I'm forgiven?'

'You'll know,' he promised.

But you didn't know. And how could God, who knew everything, ever forget your sins, anyway? Even the Bishop, who knew quite a lot, couldn't seem to forget them. You played Massenet's *Meditation* at the church Christmas concert and afterwards he patted you on the shoulder, 'Nice to see you putting your hands to good use,' he said.

You were seventeen when someone quite nice, inexplicably fell in love with you. You were so grateful and surprised, so worried he might inadvertently catch a glimpse of your grubbiness, that when he called you, '*Babe*,' and whispered, '*Please*,' you thought, why not? Your sins were already insurmountable. Any additional transgressions would only be icing on the slagheap of your unworthiness.

It hurt. He kept his eyes closed and his expression was intent throughout, as if he was praying. You felt like a voyeur. Finally you shut your eyes to allow him some privacy and while he groaned and sighed, your vacillating imagination screened scenes from your favourite romantic comedies alongside unsolicited images of bathtubs of soft, wet, worms.

You didn't confess. The next time the Bishop asked about the Law of Chastity, you lied, adding dishonesty to your other sins.

When you went away to university you stopped going to church. The library was open on Sundays and you went there instead. You borrowed romantic fiction. You looked for men whose goodness might compensate for your lack: trainee social workers, nurses, primary school teachers, but the sex was always accompanied by unwanted memories of the Bishop's thickset fingers and visions of squirming worms. Maybe the Bishop was right. Maybe you were crushed and dirty, good for nothing. You spent more and more time in library. After graduation you got a job there. You plugged the gaps in your existence with books and decided that trying on other lives would have to be enough.

Your mother sent pleading emails. 'Your decisions have eternal consequences,' she wrote. 'Why aren't you going to church? This life is a time to prepare to meet God. Don't forsake him! Whatever your trial is, you need to remember it can also be your greatest treasure.'

*

'Tell me more about the interviews,' he says.

'When we turned twelve we were interviewed twice a year. And there were extras if the Bishop thought it was necessary.'

'What happened in these interviews?'

'There were all sorts of rules and the Bishop checked up on us.'

'What kind of rules?'

'Oh, there were *loads*. Where to start? No tea, coffee or alcohol.'

He nods at your wine glass and grins.

'No clothes above the knee and no sleeveless tops.'

He lifts his pint in a toast to your bare shoulders and knees.

'No swearing, no shopping on a Sunday, no unworthy music.'

'What's unworthy music? Actually, don't bother explaining - I'm sure you've broken that rule, too.' 'No sex before marriage.'

'Ah, that one's a classic. Sex is dirty, save it for someone you love! What a mind fuck.'

'No swearing!'

He laughs. 'So what the hell could you do?'

'Not much.'

He tips his glass back and the column of his throat seesaws as he finishes his pint. 'You should write about it,' he says. 'Of course, I mean *it* not *you*. There's a difference, you know? If you take something true, a little piece of lived experience, a sort of cutting, and you plant it on the page, it can grow into fiction. That's what I think, anyway. Would you like another?'

You check your watch. 'I need to get going.'

You stand and so does he. He leans down to kiss you on the cheek. He smells of beer and skin. His gentle fingers brush your arm again, untethered and guiltless. You wonder if it might be different with him. You think about touching him back, consider turning to meet his lips, imagine unbuttoning his shirt, his belt.

'I'll look out for you next time I'm in the library,' he says. 'Well done with the publication, I'm so pleased for you!'

'Thanks.'

'Look me up in the staff directory,' he calls as you walk away. 'If you write the Treasures of Heaven story, email me - I'd love to read it.'

You pause to nod and smile and then you pick your way along the carpet, accompanied by drums, bass, and guitar. The music pounds through the warm air and into shadowy corners where couples sit at tables for two. When you reach the exit you turn to wave, but he is heading back to the bar.

Someone holds the door open and a fug of heat hits you. The light is spiky bright and you pause on the pavement to get your bearings. Pedestrians elbow past and a bus hisses as it pulls into a stop. You are spent inside, like the vessels at the exhibition. Even if your jumbly notes stretch into a story, you will never send it to anyone. You will bury it in the desk that used to belong to your grandmother, hide the ugly truth inside something beautiful.

You ease your feet out of your heels and swap them for the flip-flops in your bag. A signpost points to the station. The flip-flops slap against the hot, gum spattered pavement. You feel restless. It would be nice to run; to pick up your violin and race your fingers up and down the curves of quickly bowed arpeggios; to score a bare page with a sharpened pencil. You slide a hand into your bag and trace the spiral of your notebook - the shiny black of the railings, the cast iron lamp posts, the warm haze and the rumble of traffic will all be written into it. And so will he. You will write about a kind, married man; a man with a generous smile, a man whose touch is benediction, not invocation. Someone you will always wonder, but never worry about.

You stop to touch the railings. They are warm and slick, occasionally bumpy where the paint dribbled as it dried. You remember what he said about touching and knowing. If you close your eyes you can still feel the pattern of his stroke on your arm, still retrace the imprint of his hand with yours. You remember his gentle fingers, and you imagine keeping one in a gilded box. A relic of fear, longing and hope.

EDEN DUST

Michael Crossan

In the forest, leaf sweet darkness, a woman pleaded.

'Jesus,' she cried. Then quiet.

Against instinct, Aiden headed to the silence, afraid and alert. Old mute woods, deep night, oak and ash chromed with moon. Fennel spiced his nostrils. Soothed his dusty throat. He tasted the scent and scouted on, sleek and slow in the scrub.

On a dell bank, the woman lay limp and torn. A girl curled in the brackenfern. Aiden approached her, twig breaking steps, and her arm rose.

'No more,' she said, her eyes buried under foul swelling.

'It's all right.' Aiden knelt and lifted her head on his thigh. 'I'm here.'

'My teeth hurt.'

'You're a brave lady.'

'Still hurts.'

'Tooth fairy will fix it.'

'Funny,' she said, and her last breath spent on his arm.

A far ridge, a man loped black against the moon, a curved utensil in his hand, swinging with his stride. 'Beast,' said Aiden. He parted congealed hair from the girl's cheek. Laid her down. Stained and slack in the dirt.

Back at the tent, he retched in his sleeping bag. Sacrilege scenarios breaking his rest. Daybreak, the rain clawed, breezeless on the door mesh. Birdsong and ripe June smells. Aiden rose naked. Peed on a shrub. Squatted at a brook and shaved in the humid downpour. He towel pat his face and lit the single burner. Brewed up coffee. He poured a cupful and filled a flask. Spread jam on a raisin scone and ate it with his brew. He had planned to list his provisions but decided against an inventory in the wet. There was plenty, he was sure. Maybe a healthy week's worth. He dressed, topped a water flask, packed his rucksack, and continued up country.

Mid afternoon the rain died and the sun hurt and birds piped high on summer.

Near dusk, he picked up on a trail. A rut of trodden stems bending off through dense woods. He dropped the rucksack and studied his map and compass. The ordnance showed forestry and rivers and hills. The odd farm. Nearest town was nineteen miles west. He knelt and unclipped the rucksack. Frisked out a can of pilchards, a tin opener and fork.

Dusk cast. Sun sunk and moon thin in a lilac sky. He fastened up and followed the track. Fatigue hurting. He had been thinking of pitching for the night but felt exposed now in open plain. The path seemed recently flattened and he thought it prudent to trail it for a bit, see where it led, if anywhere.

In woodland dark he parted hickory and scanned the log cabin. A glacial moon varnished the roof in a polar hue. Smoke wicked from a brick chimney. There was a chair on the porch. A low fence squared a garden. Aiden sat under the bush and watched. The cabin looked warm, serene, a home. A candlelit window ghosted with shadow. He imagined people. Well people.

Family.

He glanced at his watch, the luminous dials at eleven. Normally he'd be camped now. He fetched a flask from his khaki trousers side pocket. Uncorked it and swigged a nod of whisky. Resumed his surveillance. Another swig, the alcohol hit. He sank in cushion leaves. Wished his wife's presence. Regrets drained him. Exhaustion crept and the flask spilled...

...Aiden hung his coat on the stand, went into the lounge, and sat on the chair opposite his wife. The lights were off, evening news flashing on the TV.

'How did it go?' she asked, lying on the couch.

'Crap. Did you take the pill?' He yanked his tie, as though the words clogged his larynx and it took a tug of the knot to free them.

'I can't.' She sat up, pulled her cardigan shut, metallic with TV light. 'It's awful.'

'Don't start.'

'I'm not ill. It would be murder.'

'Sweetheart.' Aiden stretched and touched her knee. 'It's not a person.'

She backed off along the couch. 'Of course it is.'

'It's a dot.' He slumped in the chair. Crunched his eyes and rubbed his forehead. 'A pinhead glop of cells.'

'That is so callous.'

'It's a medical fact.'

'When is it a person then?'

'Stop it.'

'Tomorrow.'

'Sweetheart.'

'Next week.'

'Enough.'

'When does it become our child?'

Aiden spanked the armrest. 'There was a mob today. A crowd for one post. Four hours, I waited. My interview stank. Nerves shat me. I'm in the bog. A lecture here, a dig there, nothing permanent.'

'You'll get a placement. You're a good lecturer.'

'I don't have the field experience. A professor said I'm a 'risk'. The panel agreed.'

'Bureaucratic sheep. Fuck them. You have the Hill Country dig.'

'That's next summer.'

'You said you wanted to be a father.' She shuffled and leaned to him. 'You said it.'

'I do.' He rubbed her thigh. 'When the time is right.'

'Don't make me do it.'

'We'll go together.'

'I can't.'

'I'll phone Dr Elliot in the morning.'

'Please don't, Aiden.'

'It's one pill. You won't know it's happened.'

'I'll know.' She folded on the couch, silent and stiff, her eyes fierce on him...

...The shotgun nozzle bunt Aiden's chest. Moonlight on his face. 'Fart and you're weed feed.' The old man wagged the single barrel and held up a rope. 'On your belly.'

'I was passing.' Aiden fumbled at his rucksack. 'I'm heading for Vinton.'

The gun cocked. 'My twelve-gauge says belly.'

'I didn't do anything.'

'Your diseased ass is on my land.'

'No.' Aiden slapped his chest. 'I'm a negative.'

The old man sniggered and stooped over him. 'You're a snake, son. Sneaking and peeping on my home. Waiting for bedtime.'

'I'm immune. I swear.'

'Sure you are. One in fifty thousand. Don't insult me, son.'

'There are six hundred negatives in Ohio. My brother told me. He was a doctor.'

'And you happen to be one of them.'

'I am.'

'That would make two on my doorstep.'

'You're immune.'

'What are the chances? Two here in the middle of nowhere.'

'Slim.' Aiden dusted nettles from his elbow. 'Say I was a virant. Doesn't make me a snake. Most are decent people.'

'Who rots decent, son?'

'Those that pass with family in their homes.'

'Hmm. It's the creepers I hate. Crawlers like you. Gutting anything that moves.'

'I've seen it.'

'Spite, that's what it is. Thrill kills before they reek.'

'I tried to help.'

'Truth is I can't tell a snake from a saint in this light.' The old man lowered the barrel at Aiden's crotch and waved the rope. 'On your guts and hands behind your back.'

'My eyes are clear.'

'Belly or buckshot.'

Aiden rolled onto his stomach, his face in the dirt. 'I'm a damned negative.'

The old man crouched, a knee on the spine, shotgun tucked under his arm. He bound Aiden's wrists. 'We'll see in the morning. A spit of pus and you're in the grave.'

The old man roped Aiden's ankles. Blew the candles and sat on the cane sofa. Gun on his lap.

Aiden fidgeted on the fireside floor. Charred logs glowing. 'A girl died in my arms.'

'It's on your shirt, son.'

'I didn't ask her name.'

'Cutters never do.'

Late night, small hours, the old man left the room. Aiden heard floorboards strain upstairs. He wrestled tight binding. Within minutes the old man returned to the sofa.

First light, he untied Aiden's ankles. Walked him to a field at gunpoint. Ordered him to kneel. Aiden knelt and the nozzle probed his back and he slumped face down in the weeds. He tasted the dew and breathed fast through his nose. The old man gripped his shoulder and hauled him round on his back. Hunkered, he stared seriously, breath wheezing, eyebrows shifting, scrutinising like a dentist. There was no pus. No yellow worm threads.

'Lord, punch me,' said the old man. He roughed Aiden's hair and turned him over and cut the rope with a knife. 'Sorry for the hassle, son.'

Up on his feet, Aiden clenched his fingers and rubbed his wrists.

The old man lowered the weapon, pouched the blade and offered his shaky palm. 'Kyle Taylor,' he said, and Aiden accepted a weak handshake.

'Aiden Cairn.'

'Good for you, son.'

'I thought you were going to shoot me.'

'I'm all talk.'

'You had me fooled.'

'I was more crapped than you.'

'What if I had been a virant?'

'I'd have blown your skull.'

Headed back to the cabin, Kyle nodded at an iron-corrugated outhouse. 'That's stacked with logs. Enough for a winter. Birch. A rare heat.' They walked beat and solemn, a fresh sun on their back, the truth blatant between them.

A moss path led to the back door. Scrapped with seeds and leaves and bark chip. The path was string tapered from vegetable patches on either side. 'Carrot and beets,' said Kyle.

Indoors, he stood the shotgun in a corner near the sink. Filled the kettle from a pail and went into the adjacent living room and put it on a grate in the hearth. He lit a few firelighters among the logs and put two mugs on the table. Spooned coffee into the mugs. They sat at the round pine table, Kyle, staring at the flame, Aiden, watching him. Kyle put on an oven glove and poured the coffee. He raised his steaming mug and studied the fire.

'Lordy,' he said, and swigged a hissy taste.

Aiden took a sip and looked down at his boots. 'Two on the doorstep,' he said, eyes fixed on catnip twined in a lace.

'What's that?' Kyle jerked as if shocked from sleep.

'Two on the doorstep.' Aiden looked at him, keeping his eye. 'You said it.'

'I did.'

'You're advanced.'

'Yellow as bile.' Kyle gazed back at the flame and his pale bottom lip trembled. He sucked a sorting breath. 'My Julia is in the dirt. I buried her two days ago. Right beside her husband, Roy, my son-in-law. I laid him the day before that. They're out back under a maple. My place is done next to theirs.'

'I'm sorry.'

'I believe you. Now believe me, there are two here on my doorstep.' Kyle took another drink and smacked his mug on the table and rose, his body a constant tremor. 'Fate's a queer master, son. Time you and Shell were acquainted.'

The cot sat under the window in a lemon room. The infant was asleep. A blanket lifting with gentle breath. 'Shell Blue,' whispered Kyle.

'A baby.'

'My granddaughter. Never wakes before eight.'

Aiden stared, squeezing the cot bars, and his breath switched rhythmic with Shell's. He felt worn and elated and his face flushed with a crimson rush. Then he took a discreet step back. Rigid and guarded. He was no warden, he thought. Cold with logic, he regretted tracking the broken stem path.

Kyle's hand crimped Aiden's shoulder. 'Did you have children?'

'No.'

'A wife.'

'Yes.'

'Me too.' He patted Aiden. 'Come on. I'll show you how to make Shell's feed.'

'What do you mean?'

'Her breakfast.'

'Why.'

'There's no wet nurse here, son.'

In the kitchen, Kyle prepared Shell's meal. He fetched a glass canister from the wall cupboard and sat it on the worktop. It was half full of fluid, and five Pyrex bottles were sunk in the bottom. Kyle tapped the container. 'Stream water. A minute from here.' He rolled up a checked shirtsleeve and dipped a hand and pulled and emptied a bottle. 'Always put a sterilising tablet in the tank.'

He opened a plastic tub and counted nine spoonfuls of powdered milk into the bottle. Poured boiled water to the nine-ounce line and screwed on the teat and shook.

'Now for the cooling.' Kyle placed the sealed bottle in a pot of cold water. 'You want it lukewarm. Tepid. Test it on the back of your hand.'

'Back of your hand?'

'Like this.' He lifted the bottle and tipped it and milk sprayed onto his clenched fist. He offered a shot to Aiden. 'Try a squirt.'

Aiden tilted the bottle. 'It's roasting,' he hissed, and blew on his hand.

'Imagine the injury to a baby's mouth.' Kyle put the bottle back in the cold pot, a puckish glint in his mucus eyes, a wily grin. 'Three minutes is just right.'

'How old is Shell?' asked Aiden, rubbing wet scorched hairs.

'Three months next Tuesday.'

'Does she eat anything apart from milk?'

'Good question.' Kyle scratched a floss of gray above his left ear. 'Shell's on four nine-ounce feeds a day. Every three hours. Try feeding her half a rusk in a week or two.'

'Me.' That harsh logic again. A rusty thirst. The urge to flee.

'You, son.' After a short quiet, Kyle said, 'Mix the rusk into her bottle. Before the cooling. Only her morning feed for the first few days.'

'What's rusk?'

'Cereal biscuit. Melts in hot milk.'

'You're claiming my life.'

'I'm begging Shell's.'

Kyle lifted the kettle and eased the spout in the water pail. Glugged half full, he put it on the hearth and stoked the flame with an iron poker. He added two logs from a bucket. 'Shell's colicky so don't rush it,' he said, and sleeved sweat from his forehead. 'When she keeps down her breakfast add rusk to her night feed. Gradually introduce more solids and cut down on the milk. Soft cereal, mushy carrot and potato, creamed rice, that type of thing.'

'We need to discuss this.'

'Time's a mugger, son. And I'm jumped.' Kyle arched breathy and touched his back. Pinched his kidney. 'Shell's room is stacked with everything she needs. Clothes, nappies, toiletries. There's a ton of stuff in the basement.'

'I've never held a baby.'

'Shell's tame as a foal. She doesn't fuss. And every provision is here. Years of stock. Salt, sugar, flour, pasta, cereal, rice, tins. Most type of vegetable seed. We have dried meats, dried fruits, jams, honey, marmalade, powdered milk and powdered egg. Powdered egg is best scrambled. The basement's a larder. And there are plenty boxes of matches and candles.'

'I'm going southwest.'

'Why.'

'There's a commune in Vinton.'

'Ah. The Green Brigade.'

'Something like that. There are maybe forty of them.'

Wheezy and frail, Kyle sat in the fireside chair. 'Living off the prairie,' he said, and kicked a log into the flame with his boot heel. 'God country.'

'They grow crops. Some hunt. There are a few anglers. I'm an archaeologist. I worked on a dig in the Hill Country last summer. Spent a month camping with them.'

'A bone digger. You don't look like one.'

'How's that? What does an archaeologist look like?'

'Old. Decrepit like me. You're hardly twenty.'

'Twenty-six.'

'You'd never know it.'

'So I've heard.'

'Bone digger camper, eh.'

'I like camping. At least I used too.'

'Dump a turd and bury it,' said Kyle. 'Your gear is quality. I'll hand you that.'

'Good equipment lasts a lifetime.'

'It's packed under the basement stair, by the way.'

'Thanks.'

'I know quality when I see it.'

'Can't cheat on winter.'

'You camped in those remote places in winter?'

'I liked the solitude. Me and the elements and the bones.'

'And you think because the greenies lived outside the herd they survived.'

'It's possible.'

'Hmm.'

'You don't think it's feasible.'

'It's unlikely.'

'They're cut off. Miles from anyone.'

Sat up straight, Kyle's arm carved an arc in the air. 'This cabin was a hunting lodge. My father built it. Six summers of muscle and sweat. Access is from the river. Trees cram the banks. You can't see the cabin from there. I doubt anyone knows this place exists.'

'There's another route. I found it, remember.'

'Lordy knows how. Out back, sycamores hide us. And our front is red oak and hills. Thousands of acres.' Kyle coughed and dredged and spat into the flames. He settled in the chair. 'God's own must often stumble into God Country.'

'I'm hardly God's own. There was a path cut through the woods.'

'That would be the kids. I warned them about leaving tell trails. Julia and Roy were hikers. Fresh-air addicts. Trust me, son. Few have trampled the grass here.'

'How did you transport the supplies?'

'Roy's boat.' Kyle bent and speared logs with the poker. 'Sailed nine weeks ago. During the outbreak in Mexico. A Catana catamaran.'

'Boating's not my thing.'

'It's a yacht. Thirty-three footer.'

'Big boat.'

'Big enough. We got everything up in one trip.'

'Where did you get the fuel? The pumps were dead long before Mexico.'

'Julia sniffed global during Korea's quarantine. Biblical. She drove town to town in the jeep. Topped a wagonload of jerry cans and stored them in her cellar.'

'Smart lady.'

'Sharp as a spike. The boat's moored, hidden in a cove.'

'What's your grouch with Vinton?'

'No grouch. I wish your greenies nothing but mercy. But you don't get more remote than here.' Kyle put on the oven gloves and lifted the steaming kettle and poured the coffee. 'The virus came from the sky, son. The roof fell on everyone.'

After his coffee, Kyle checked on Shell. She was sound. Safe in sleep. He idled at the cot. 'Child,' he whispered. 'You have a life.'

He slouched back to his chair. 'I'm bagged, son.'

Aiden stood quiet at the window watching the sky. Miles of blue. His empathy hurt. Veins spate with emotion. The old man felt like kin.

'Shell is yours now. Your own.'

'She's beautiful.'

Bunked in the chair, Kyle closed his eyes and blew. Rattle breath. 'Lordy, son.'

Aiden went into the kitchen and scooped water from the pail with a pot and rinsed out the mugs at the sink. He tried the taps. A dry judder, like a truck braking, not a drip. He turned off the taps and checked on Kyle over his shoulder. The old man was snoring, chin on chest, hands spread on his flat belly. Sunrays forked through the window. Pasted his gouged face. Aiden thought he resembled a serene youth.

'Lord, punch me,' he said in tribute, and he went out the back door.

Rope burns welt his wrists. He loosened the watchstrap a notch. Checked the time. Near ten past six. Guessed he had been up since five. He wolfed berry air. Face lifted at the lake sky. The sore sun. Sleepless nights on his back, he felt worn to the marrow and strolled through the sycamores to the river. He saw the boat in a spruce inlet. On a reed bank he sat on a log and looked out over the sun starry calm. Birdsong all to himself.

Walking up the back path, Aiden smelt the rot. Early sweet decay. He knew it would sour rancid in the heat. Same odour as the streets and malls. Hospitals and churches. Town halls and city halls. The same vile ferment of his wife.

Squat and flexed, he linked hands around Kyle's waist and rose with him belly down over his right shoulder. The weight of a boy. He carried him out the back door, past a broccoli crop toward two grass mounds and a slope of earth with a spade stumped like a mast. Under the maple he stood in the grave and laid the old man on his back. He took off his shirt, spread it on the grey wax face, filled in the grave, and stood head bowed quiet.

'Lordy, Kyle,' he said, and saluted the dirt.

After a wash at the stream, he went back to the cabin and sat in the fireside chair. Kyle's shape was in the seat. Aiden shifted and fitted and watched the smoky logs. A green flame danced and he thought about Shell, on whether Kyle could have taken her, and of her horror if he couldn't. As he mused over this, the child began to cry.

'Hello, miss.' Aiden leaned over the cot and Shell stopped crying. 'You smell.'

Treacle-brown eyes shone and sussed him. He touched her cheek. Tiny fingers wrapped his pinkie. 'Shit,' he cried, snapping his hand away.

Shell jumped. Squashed her face and squealed.

'Shit.' Aiden circled her cot, hands messing his hair. 'Shit, shit, shit.'

She tensed and shivered and bawled.

'You got lungs like a whale.' Aiden bent and fondled her ear. 'Moby Dame.'

Touch and words calmed her. 'You're stuck with me,' hushed Aiden. 'Let's sort you.'

It was a task undressing her. Shell kicked and slapped and wailed. The babygro was damp and warm. Unclipped and removed, Aiden peeled the diaper tabs. He tugged the nappy, swabbing her soiled bottom with dry folds of the padding. Twice he turned away for a clean breath. Glad the procedure was obvious; he wrapped and binned the spongy lump in a plastic bucket.

He held her in a crooked arm. Lifted a gown from the dresser and wriggled it onto her as he skirted the stairway to the living room. He had no clue to the order of things, but the way she gnawed her knuckles he thought it wise to prioritise her food. He kept her in one arm, her back against his bare chest, and fetched the prepared bottle from the pot. Shell seemed to elongate. Her eyes widened, mouth gaped; her arms and legs stretched starfish. She booted and reached and vibrated at her feed.

'Tame as a foal, Kyle.' Aiden stumbled to the couch and offered the teat.

Her eyes scrunched into teary slits and her head turned from side to side. When the teat was here, her mouth was there, and she yelled trembling feral.

[38]

'Take it, lady,' said Aiden, trying to catch her. Milk leaked and ran with her tears. Elbows paddling, he persevered and her mouth claimed the elusive prize.

'Bravo.' He wiped her chin with a fingertip. 'What a performance.'

Quick tremors shook Shell's small frame. She gulped loud and fast and her wet eyes focused on Aiden. Instinctively, he kissed her forehead. A gush of bubbles rushed in the bottle. She had stopped feeding. Aiden winked and she smiled. A fleeting favour.

Serious again on her breakfast, Shell watched him, her palm folded on his thumb, and Aiden was at once her keeper.

FINISHED

SARAH BOWER

Charlotte is finished. She has a mediocre degree from a respectable university in something like art history or English literature. She has completed courses in cordon bleu cookery and flower arranging, and has toured the galleries of Tuscany and Rome, and, if she was moved by anything she saw, she has kept it, quite properly, to herself. Charlotte has even learned how to climb out of the passenger seat of a low-slung sports car, wearing a short skirt, without revealing her underwear. She is finished.

At university, in Durham or, perhaps, Warwick, she has met Bob. Bob is a second year when she arrives, fresh from the hockey pitches on which the diplomatic wives and colonels' ladies of Empire were trained in bygone times. Although they are attracted to one another from the outset, and share a slow dance at the Freshers' disco hosted by the tennis club, they agree not to start dating until the year end exams are over. Bob is studying law, or economics; behind his burgundy loons and cheesecloth shirt you can, if you look carefully, already see the pinstripe suit; his neck, when Charlotte sweeps away his long, blond curls on the morning after the first night they spend together in his dope-and joss-stick-smelling room, is all ready for the raw, plucked goose look it will wear for most of his life, courtesy of the barber next door to the law courts who used to cut his father's hair.

Once Charlotte is finished, her father pulls a few strings to get her a little job in PR, or as a medical secretary. She rents a house in a harmlessly bohemian part of town with a couple of girls she was at university with. She uses a legacy from her grandmother to buy herself a little runabout, a little space where no-one can reach her and she can listen to David Bowie singing Wild is the Wind over and over again without anyone accusing her of being sentimental, or wanting what girls like her can never have. On Saturdays, the girls give dinner parties; they woo the earnest young men who bring them flowers and Chianti, or tickets to see Pink Floyd, with big bowls of spaghetti Bolognese, fresh herbs and diced chicken livers mixed into the sauce, and chocolate mousse. They eat seated on the floor around the coffee table. The crockery is mismatched and there is never enough cutlery or glasses, but this does not deter the girls from doing things 'properly', serving several courses and different wines with each, draping the table with white linen and bedecking their shabby sitting room with candles and stiff carnation sprays. They are in their early twenties; they still believe that what they see of their mothers is the truth.

Within a year, Charlotte and Bob are engaged. Bob is offered a partnership and a wedding date is set. Charlotte wears Gina Fratini. Photographed in her father's rose garden, she is radiant. Snapped on honeymoon in Rhodes, she glows, as if the Aegean sun, and salads of fat, bright tomatoes and glossy olives, and the young, yellow, slightly fizzing wine are shining from inside her. There'll be a honeymoon baby, mark my words, say various friends and neighbours of their parents, invited to look at the slides.

It is the first time Charlotte's life has failed to go to plan. Though she smiles as she paints the small back room of her new married home, and pastes up an alphabet frieze, inside she seethes with resentment against her body. She feels it has betrayed her. How could it not know the script? How could it, after twenty four years of assiduous training, fail to realise that its role was to remain toned, lovely in its clothes and alluring to Bob out of them, for two or three more years before letting itself go in an orgy of fecundity?

She says nothing to Bob about her feelings but keeps them within, with the growing baby. Perhaps that is why she feels so sick all the time and can eat nothing but dry cornflakes for weeks. But Bob is so excited, stroking her swollen breasts and the waxing moon of her belly with a fresh, wide-eyed wonder that carries her back to the early days of their courtship. As does the arousal she feels, almost permanently, so she counts the hours until she will hear his key in the latch, spends the afternoons, when the nausea recedes, preparing little amuses bouche, hard-boiled quails' eggs, bite-size tartes aux fraises, mini lasagnes and onion bhajis, that she can feed him in bed once she is sated, full of sex, and growing baby, and anger.

Her figure is back to normal within weeks of the birth of her son, though Bob's belly is potting a little, as if the pregnancy isn't over but has simply transferred itself from her to him. She finds this funny. Bob doesn't. She finds within herself, when nursing her baby, a fierce, protective love for which she was not trained on the playing fields of Cheltenham, or Roedean, a love which tears at her, leaving her ragged as a broken nail. It makes her realise that what she feels for Bob is not love, was never love, was no more than some kind of Pavlovian conditioning. (It is always possible Charlotte studied psychology at university, or sociology. It is possible that Charlotte is serious, and intelligent.)

Bob works longer hours at the office, goes drinking with colleagues afterwards. He spends Saturdays at the golf club. He has to, he explains to Charlotte. It is all part of getting on, and he has to get on now he has a family to support. Charlotte knows he is right; besides, she has read in her books on parenting that even tiny babies are sensible to tensions between their parents. She goes to mother and baby group, to baby gym and baby swimming, and Jazzercise and tennis. She makes new friends, other young women who are at home with their children. They take turns to entertain one another to lunch – the latest Delia for the mothers, homemade shepherds' pie for the toddlers, miniature cartons of apple juice and wine boxes from Stowells of Chelsea. As lunch sometimes extends into the cocktail hour, they meet one another's husbands, solid, good humoured men who can shrug off a raincoat, put down a briefcase and produce a tray of gin and tonics in a single, fluid movement.

On Saturday nights, there are dinner parties, and now they are all married couples there are matching sets of crockery and cutlery, crystal glasses for everything from Perrier to port, starched snow-drifts of table linen. New classic dishes appear in the repertoire, involving goats cheese and balsamic vinegar and kiwi fruits. Wine is as often Chilean or Australian as French. Holidays are taken in Florida and Bali as well as Italy and Spain. The world is shrinking to the size of a dinner table laid for eight. Charlotte smokes, and watches Bob scoop and shovel and hack his way through mousses and flans and platters of interesting English cheeses.

Charlotte keeps her eyes open and stares at the mole on Bob's left shoulder that she used to kiss, as he toils above her, his pores exuding garlic and brandy, savouring his final dish on a Saturday night. And in due course, when their son is two, Charlotte gives birth to a daughter. The arrival of her daughter awakens a new kind of ferocity in Charlotte, something altogether colder and more ruthless than the love that overwhelmed her when her son was born. Now she understands the boarding school, the courses in cookery and flower arranging, the 'improving' trips to the cul-tural hothouses of Europe. Now she knows what she was finished for and that her own daughter will never be finished.

The years pass. The children grow, and are sent to the schools their parents attended. The sensitive kids, who cried at night and ran away, and hid under pianos in music rooms to avoid games, and the hale bullies with their shelves of silverware for cricket and rugby, the teenagers who choked on their Number Sixes be-hind the bike sheds and enjoyed their first, awkward snogs at school dances, are all together now on boards of governors, all joined in the conspiracy to persuade their own children that their school days will be the best of their lives. The slow earthquake of divorce and remarriage has begun, but, though the foundations of their marriage shiver sometimes, Charlotte and Bob keep their footing, keep their heads and carry on. Charlotte feels like a plan-et trapped in an ancient orbit, whose path crosses Bob's at certain predetermined times, on family holidays, at Christmas lunch, in due course at graduation ceremonies, and weddings, and when their grandchildren are born. She is not discontented. Her orbit is inevitable. She is finished.

When the ground beneath her feet cracks, it is the last thing she expects. She is visiting an exhibition with some members of her NADFAS group, standing alone before a small sculpture in pink-veined marble, a plump woman, sleeping, curled on her side, her head pillowed on one voluptuous arm, her belly sagging slightly, a fleshy hammock. It is this which has aroused Charlotte's feeling for the piece, her sense that the relationship between the sculptor and his model is one of deep affection and secret humour.

'What do you think?'

Charlotte starts.

'I'm sorry. I shouldn't have interrupted you.'

She turns. At first she is looking at a throat, and a shadow of dark hair above the open collar of a lilac coloured shirt. The man who has spoken is very tall. Raising her eyes, she says, 'Not at all,' and, before she even knows what is going to come out of her mouth, 'No-one has asked me what I think for about thirty years. I think.' She laughs. He laughs. His front teeth overlap slightly and his eyes are sea-green.

'It's just that…I'm the sculptor.'

She finds out the model was his mother. She finds out he is interested in what she thinks, about everything, from movies to vegetable growing, politics to puddings. She remembers she loves Westerns, and Joni Mitchell, and Batman, and Mozart's operas. She remembers how, as a little girl, before she was finished, she loved to bake, standing on a stool at the counter beside her mother, swathed in a too-big apron and lost in a haze of flour and icing sugar; how she baked to express the love that was in her, the way he made his sculpture. Her body remembers sex; it seems to remember the tall sculptor's weight, the shape of his mouth and the touch of his scarred hands, and the excitement of clandestine meetings that makes it sing like a harp string.

Yet the year the sculptor was born was the same year she lost her virginity.

He asks her why she married. He himself has never been able to see the point of it. His own parents are divorced. She wants to tell him she married, and has stayed married, so her children will not be damaged as he is. He has a true heart, she believes, but its truth is chipped and misshapen, a failed sculpture. But instead she tells him the truth, that she married because it was expected of her, and has stayed married because she doesn't know what else to do. Her marriage has all the right ingredients, carefully measured, but somehow, they have never blended. Perhaps something wasn't quite fresh enough to begin with, perhaps the oven door was opened too soon. Her marriage is sustaining, but not tasty. You have baked yourself, says the sculptor, licking dark chocolate off her tongue in a bed which has four posters and white curtains and belongs to neither of them, into a bit of a pie.

When the sculptor leaves her, she is sad, even though he does it kindly and she always knew it couldn't last. She consoles herself with baking, throws herself into making cookies and cupcakes, muffins and sponges, barm cakes and teabreads and fresh cream gateaux. She bakes for her children, for charity cake stalls and cricket teas. She bakes for love. Whenever she and Bob are invited out to dinner she takes gifts of tiny brownies or white chocolate truffles. Her tiered cake tin is always stuffed with good things and Bob, despite his blood pressure and cholesterol, cannot help dipping into it, now he is retired. Charlotte brings him biscuits with his morning coffee when he takes a break from the garden. A slice of cake accompanies his afternoon tea when he comes in from the bowls club. Last thing in the evening, after Charlotte has gone to bed, he has a glass of milk and something sweet to settle him for the night. She knows this because he leaves his glass and plate in the sink; she wonders why he cannot put them in the dishwasher but she never asks; the answer would not interest her.

'He wouldn't have known a thing about it,' says the doctor in the hospital's family room. 'Massive heart attack.'

'On the sixteenth as well,' adds Charlotte's son, his arm about her shoulders. Her daughter is not there. Her daughter works in Afghanistan, for a charity that defends the rights of women. Charlotte smiles at her son, who has spoken from the heart as he always does. The sixteenth was Bob's favourite hole. And the heart, Charlotte sees now, in this room whose walls hum faintly with all the life-changing words that have been exchanged within them, may be without adornment, like her son's, or battered as the sculptor's, but it is never finished. Charlotte is not finished.

She is in a seaside town in South America, or North Africa, when she sees the sculptor again. She is sitting in the window of a coffee shop, writing postcards to her grandchildren, when she spots him across the street, leaning one elbow against the sea wall and sketching in a pad. There is grey in his beard, she observes, and he has put on weight. She wonders if his mother is still alive, if he has ever married, where the small marble is now that made her fall in love with him. She hopes that perfect, finished, loving thing has the home it deserves. Draining her cup, she calls for her bill and leaves, choosing her path away from the sea because she can. There is nowhere particular she has to be.

Charlotte no longer cooks, has forgotten entirely how to arrange flowers or make a soufflé and does not lead the kind of life that involves sports cars or short skirts. Charlotte is far from finished.

VIOLET

BARNABY WALSH

Thieving the lead from a church roof, high up on top of this St Jerome's, Ryan pauses and spits: the gob catches the moonlight, falls and vanishes into the graveyard's darkness below. Ryan and his uncle Dean working together in the night to strip the church of its ancient lead, peeling off great slabs of the stuff and lowering them by rope to the ground, where Dean's mate loads them into the church's own wheelie bins to roll them to the van. It's only a small village, far out of town. There are the dark windows of the vicarage nearby, a crooked row of houses, the odd shop, a pub, nothing beyond for miles but empty fields, and thick woods rising behind the churchyard's slope of graves. Not much chance of being spotted, if they're stealthy-like. If anyone asks we're just admiring the view, Dean says – can't prove we're not, can they?

From up here the town's lights are all laid out for Ryan, twinkling in the pollution the way stars don't anymore. One of the dark patches between the lights of one of those tower blocks is home: his mum and baby brother asleep by now, if the baby isn't screaming; if his mum isn't lying awake, worrying about him. Not knowing where he is. And somewhere below the lit disc of the town hall's clock tower is the library, where he can't go anymore. Or if he did set foot he knows he'd only end up knocking down bookshelves or something, dominoing them down all over the place ...

then they really wouldn't let him back. He'll never use his library card again. Though it's fucked up enough that he has one in the first place, even if it does have someone else's name on it, and it isn't like he ever borrowed a book – he only used to go for the free internet, 'cause they've not got a computer at home, not since the old one died: Ryan's mum would never accept one of Dean's nicked ones. Plus there's his baby brother's howling to get away from. The library's just a place to go. Not got a job to go to, since leaving school almost two years ago, only a couple things he quickly got himself sacked from. The internet at least he can fuck about on. Later he went mainly to stare at this girl who worked there Saturdays. Saturdays and some holidays – she was still at school, he'd guessed. A part-time job, extra pocket money.

Her name was Violet, he overheard once, though when she told it him herself he pretended not to know. She didn't work the library's computer desk, was always off over where the books lived. Once he followed her for a bit, as she wandered the walls of books, pretending he was interested in what words might say, trying to catch glimpses of her through the spaces between shelves. He hid his mobile behind a book, poked its eye over the top and tried to take sneaky little photos of her. Till he accidentally glanced at some lines on the page: poetry. It'd freaked him out: he dropped the book and ran. He worried afterwards: what if she'd heard the fall, seen him legging it, picked up the book … poetry, fuck, what'd it make her think of him? Fuck. And all he found he'd caught on the camera was blurred angles of ceiling, carpet, his thumb's edge, books…

Finally it was Uncle Dean's long-planned escapade that gave Ryan the thought, an excuse to talk to her. An excuse in his head. One Saturday he worked up his courage with a little vodka, and by clenching his fists and shouting at himself in the mirror of the library's gents. An old man appeared behind him, watched a moment, backed silently out again. Ryan punched at the mirror, stopped his fist a millimetre from shattering it, then went and found her. She was standing with her face bent into a book, the top of her head touching the row of still more of the things, books, on the shelf before her. She wore purple tights, and a black dress that bared much of her back. He watched her a minute, the scattering of freckles on her nape: she didn't move, not at all. Silver clips with green stones kept her hair from falling on the page. She was still, like a ghost. Fucking reading. Another minute; she turned a page, only that. Then he went to her, before he'd to screw up his courage all over again.

'Hey,' he said.

She looked up from the book, blinking as she surfaced from the words, from whatever world they'd taken her to, then hesitated as she gazed at him, bemusedly, as if she knew but couldn't quite place him.

'Hello?' she said.

'A book,' he said, 'there's a book I'm after. 'Cause this is a library, yeah? Where you get books, yeah?'

'Ye-es,' she said, looking round at all the loaded shelves as if to be sure. Looks like it to her.

'And so you can find me one, yeah?'

'Okay,' she said with a little gulp, glancing from side to side as if it were something she'd never tried before, and probably against the rules – taking the piss, Ryan could tell, but not unkindly. Her eyes were a very pale grey, he saw, and felt for a moment obscurely frightened. 'Any in particular?'

'About … uh, church roofs?'

'Church roofs?'

'Yeah, you know. Church … things and bits. Bits of churches. With pictures.'

'You mean, what, architecture? Church architecture?'

Not what she'd expected: legal advice must've looked more likely. Criminal law. Loads of time yet for that. But okay then – she shrugged off a little laugh, snapped shut her book and shelved it, and bent her finger for him to follow her deeper into the books… He hung back warily behind her, but over her shoulder she smiled:

'Don't let them see you're frightened,' she said, still moving, holding out a hand behind her as if for him to take. 'That's how they get you.'

As she disappeared round a corner he plunged after her, into the dark again, high walls of shelves looming. She led him zigzagging between all the stacks of all the books he'd never read. He hurried to keep up, his eyes on the sharp wings of her shoulder blades, and when she stopped abruptly he walked into her. She pushed him off with a nervous giggle, and started drawing books off shelves and dumping them in his arms, reading him the titles. Churches and cathedrals on the covers, books Dean'd only spit at. Already Ryan couldn't really be bothered anymore to pretend he was interested. But Violet would do all the pretending they needed.

'You used to go to my school, didn't you?' she asked out of nowhere, confusing him. He stared at a book's cover: a gargoyle scowled back at him, and he could've mistook it for the mirror again. He'd not known he should know her. Couldn't imagine it. 'Don't recognise me? Why would you? I was only second year when you left. You were a bit famous, though. I did think it was a bit harsh, when they kicked you out – after all it's not like you killed anyone, is it? But then again, maybe it was probably what you wanted – you were never there much anyway, were you? I've never been brave enough to do that, to just not go. Anyway, churches. Why the sudden book-urges?'

He grunted something, shrugged a shoulder. Let her be the one who talks. He saw how nervous she was, how nervous he was making her, and saw too that for some reason she'd decided not to run away from him. He saw that. And then something happened that his brain skipped somehow, though he tried to reconstruct it later, lying in bed, mentally recycling the day, hoping that if she was all that was in his mind as he fell asleep she'd follow him into dreams. But he couldn't retrace any detail – he had one mental image of her, books under her arm, dragging him after her by the hand. Holding his hand. And then there was a kind of mental sneeze, and he was in the library's café with this big bastard book of churches in his lap, and she was beside him and leaning against him to point something out, pointing at a picture, at some little nook in a map of a church, and he could smell her hair and feel her breast against his arm, and he was glad of the book in his lap because he needed something to hide behind.

It'd been late in the afternoon when he'd got there, the library not too far from closing: another member of staff came and told them, time to fuck off. Violet rushed off to check out some of the books on her card; Ryan went and stood outside, lightly kicking a wall, his hands in his pockets. He pulled his hood up over his shaven head. He knew what he looked like. And felt secretly, strangely pleased with himself: no one'd guess that he was waiting for a girl with books. But then Violet took ages: she was waiting for him to be gone, he decided, before she'd come out, so she wouldn't have to see him again. He didn't know what exactly he'd done, or what it was about him, but he knew there'd been something. Across the road on a bench some girls giggled together, nudging one another: he felt their eyes on him. He turned to go, was almost at the corner before Violet's arm materialised under his, and his name on her lips. She had her coat on, and her hood pulled up too against rain that hadn't come yet.

'Walk me to the bus stop, then,' she said. Surprised, he looked in her eyes and saw again in them the nervousness visible beneath her confidence, nervousness at being with him. She was scared of him. But still she was there. They walked, and neither spoke till they got to the bus and he thrust his mobile at her and said, 'Put your number in that,' knowing she'd have to, whether she was having second thoughts or not.

*

He called her a couple of days later, with no idea what to say, but it was all right, she came up with something: she'd been looking at the books she'd picked out for him and then taken for herself, they were really interesting, she'd like to show him some things, come round tomorrow, here's my address. He could hear in her voice how little she knew what she was doing, and how much that excited her. The thing with the churches – he'd started it, but it was all her keeping it up – was so stupid he didn't even say anything. He hung up.

Her house turned out to be a fuck-off great detached thing, double-garaged, a big heap of tree nodding over its lawn; he felt as if someone'd call the police just for him walking up the street. Why the fuck had she even asked him here? Someone like him. He was deciding vaguely that she must be a bit mad, and also that that was okay. Mad. Asking for it. He hoped she was and was frightened by it as well.

'My long-lost Ryan!' Violet said excitedly as she opened the door, as if she'd known him forever but he'd been gone for ages. She kept saying things as if something, as if she weren't quite in the same world as him. He didn't think about it. He was in her house, it was dark. It was a weekday, now, chosen because her parents were out. She was still in school uniform, but barefoot. He hesitated a bit and then showed her the weed he had in his pocket, bought off his uncle Dean, with no family discount at all, to make it easier to talk. Violet's eyes widened. He'd really not got much idea what he was doing there, though he did reckon, dimly, that he was part of some self-conscious going-off-the-rails thing she was doing, experimentally. Trying to upset her parents; good middle-class girl for once in her life being bad. For some reason. Little bit of a rebellion. Only she was a bit crap at it, maybe. That's what he reckoned, though what was in her head he'd never be able to tell. No, he couldn't. But he could really fucking hurt her, he realised, and his brain went light, emptied.

As they'd come up the stairs there'd been no sign of other life, the rest of the house dark; pictures on the walls of her as a little girl, of her parents, no sisters or brothers. At the end of the dark corridor was a mirror; moving towards it, they watched each other watch each other. Then this door was her bedroom's: it was very neat, bookish, bare like a cell. There was a fucking clarinet – she had to tell him what it was called – propped in a corner, but no posters on the walls, no photos of family or friends or anything like decoration. Her computer's screen dark.

She'd never smoked anything before, she told him, and he could see her getting high just watching him roll a joint. They sat on her bed, leant against the wall. Books spread about them. He eyed the window, seeing himself having to jump out of it if the parents came home early.

Their fingers touched as he passed her the spliff. The weed made her talkative. She doesn't actually work at the library, why'd he think that? Okay, so she's there all the time. She's a book-girl.

She volunteers too at the little kids' reading group, and with the disabled kids that come there.

'What, those retards?'

'Learning difficulties, thought you'd empathise.'

'What?'

She took a puff on the joint: she coughed, a fist to her lips, screwed up her watering eyes. She laughed and tried again.

She was fourteen, insanely clever ... he got a little frightened again, listening to her brains. Twelve A's she was chasing in her GCSEs, she told him, A's with stars on, and she'd get them, too. It would have been thirteen, only her mum was a bit superstitious since her dad died, and wouldn't let her. For GCSEs Ryan got – let him think – well, three, and the grades were vowels but not A's. Even though he'd got kicked out of school, his mum'd made him sit the exams: fuck lot of good that did. A-levels for her, afterwards, of course, then university... The trajectory of her life upwards, while Ryan's only really good times'd been at school. Or, more usually, not at school when he'd been meant to be there. No one messed with him back then, he'd've kicked the shit out of them; a right cocky little twat he'd been. But weird how quiet life'd got since then, some days he hardly spoke at all.

He sat there listening to her with his hand on her thigh; somehow he'd managed to do that, the hem of her skirt resting lightly on his knuckles. After a bit he more or less tuned out the words as she spoke, just watched her lips move, talking, sucking occasionally on the spliff, though he had most of it – she didn't need much – her gaze off through the wall, as she told him now about something that'd fascinated her in one of the books she'd checked out on her own card after Ryan's fake interest had wilted. She showed him the pictures, these people called anchorites or anchoresses who got bricked up in little rooms in church walls for all their lives just to be given over to religious devotion, can you imagine that?

'No,' he said. 'My imagination won't do what I want.'

'Oh, that's so sad!' she said, and clapped her hands silently together as if in delight.

By then he'd worked his hand up her shirt, and into her bra. She didn't seem to have noticed, just kept talking, looking at the books pooled about them on the bed or staring at the wall, the joint now gone. She hadn't opened the window. Her breast was warm and new, cupped in his palm. This was going well till something made her suddenly jump up from the bed and dash to the window. His hand caught in her bra, she dragged him up a little along with her, till he yanked it free and fell back onto the bed. He sat there, watching her as she stood at the window.

'An ambulance,' she said, leaning forwards on the glass. 'Did you hear? I can't see its blue. They frighten me now when I see them. Whenever one passes me I have to do this like little mental prayer for whoever might be in it. It's not even like I believe in God or anything, but I was scared once and did it once for my dad and even if it didn't work that time, ever since then I've had to do this little like psychic wordless mental prayer, it's a compulsion. And because I thought what if it does work sometimes, and just in case it does I have to do it for every other ambulance I see, how could you leave someone out? It's just like a wish, that they be all right, but so now I'm sort of starting to get a teeny bit obsessed, a little bit. Always watching for them. My friends say I'm mad, or they would if I had any.'

By then Ryan was at the window with her. Throughout her long nervy speech a kind of anger had been rising in him. He wanted to end all this bollocks she was talking. Words, fucking words. He felt like punching her, and he could do it, he could just fucking do it – punch a teenage girl in the face, feel her nose crumpling under his knuckles. He felt this great stillness inside himself, held in by clenched fists, that he wanted just to shatter forever.

Instead she kissed him. Gently her eyes closed and her lips moved onto his. They stood like that a moment, and then he moved into the kiss instead: he took her head, so small and delicate, into his hands; he pushed his tongue into her mouth.

After a little she pulled back a bit. 'Don't be so aggressive,' she said. Telling him as if this was his first kiss, not hers. 'Here,' she said, and sat him back down on the edge of the bed. 'Gently. Like this.' And her lips moved lightly on his, her tongue's tip gently touched his. 'That's nice,' she said. Her wrists in his hands now so thin, so snappable; her fingers so small, twined in his. Ryan slid his hand up her thin thigh again, pushing up her skirt. She allowed it a moment before gently smilingly saying, 'No.' He shrugged, used his hands instead to roll another joint. Violet sat watching him, gone quiet at last. A little while after this one was finished, she crawled away from him, curled herself up on top of the pillow and slept. Ryan watched her. Did she know he was still there? I could really hurt her, he thought again, but this time the thought was dead. Long girlish snores, delicate and quiet. Ryan sat alone at the foot of the bed. He looked at her; he looked at the walls, the window, the clock. Her cell. She'd told him he would have to be gone by ten; it was forty minutes past. The bed creaked as he got up. He stood over her. Reached out his hand and stopped it just from touching her face. Her eyes closed, and he thought that secretly she was awake, really, and wanting him to touch her. This'd be what she wants. She was curled up, bare legs folded to her chest. He pulled out his mobile, took a picture or two of her with it. Zoomed in on her face, her lips; pulled back to take in her legs. He wanted to touch her legs again, her breasts, face, lips; knew he couldn't right now. But told himself he would again, one day, one day not a million miles away.

He pulled the bedclothes up to cover her; she shifted, made small noises with her lips – he leaned close again, listening for his name. She was still. Slept on. He saw paper on her desk and thought to leave a note, but didn't know what to write, and didn't like to think of her seeing the state of his handwriting, his spelling. Text messages don't need writing. He could send one, any time; could call her, even. It was what he was meant to do. She was his girlfriend. He had a girlfriend.

He sneaked out quietly, before her parents got home. She'd said something about her dad, but he'd forgot what it was. Something about him being a nutter? Ryan wondered if her dad hit her. He could do something about that, Ryan could. As he walked up the road a car passed, the woman driving it glancing at him: Violet's mother, maybe. If only she knew. If only anyone knew. Little explosions in his heart: hope, after all. A surprise, that. Later, wandering home in the dark, in the faint drizzle getting slowly but totally piss-soaked through because he'd not brought his jacket, his

T-shirt clinging wetly to his skin and his trainers sodden, still with the virginity he'd hoped to be shed of and a pain in his bellend from his hard-on pressing on his jeans, still he felt like ripping off his T-shirt and howling at the moon. The rain on him like some kind of baptism, rebirth, whatever, fuck it, fuck everything else, he was in love.

*

As the sun was rising he finally fell asleep; it was past its height as he woke. He couldn't recall any dreams, didn't think to wonder about them. The light through his bedroom's thin curtains was oddly ordinary. Naked, he opened the window to lean out over the nine storeys, the wind better than a shower. It wasn't supposed to open so far, but the safety thing was broken. Bracing himself with his gut against the windowsill, he leaned forwards, forwards... He brought himself to the point of falling and then stopped: any farther and... He leaned back in, shut the window.

He wandered into the kitchen. His mum'd left a mug for him on the kitchen counter, with a teabag and spoon in it – as if he couldn't get that far on his own. He switched the kettle on. Folded and propped against the sugar bowl was a note for him: Ryan, it said in his mum's loopy handwriting. He pretended not to see it, tried to act normal but without his eye falling that way. But then the letters were too big, he couldn't pretend, he unfolded it. Number 1: Do the hoovering. Number 2: Get yourself down the job centre today, for God's and yours and all our sakes. 'Shit,' he said aloud. He looked around for something to break, but stopped himself. Three: Go collect your brother's repeat prescription. DO NOT FORGET. 'Little bastard,' said Ryan. The note ended: Love, Mum xxx. The last words like her fingers stroking his hair. But his head was shaved almost to the bone, prickly to his mum's touch, or Violet's. And then there was: PS. If your uncle Dean rings up again, hang straight up on him. Don't even talk to him. If he turns up here, DO NOT LET HIM IN THE FLAT. If he won't go away, call me, call the police. Ignore him. M x.

Too late, too late. Ryan got out his phone and read again Dean's last text, reminding himself where they were meeting, so he'd not forget. Dean'd kill him if he forgot. Dean, long since black-sheeped from the family, but who'd never quite go away.

And then in the kitchen a thing happened that sometimes happened. As he poured boiling water into the mug, onto the teabag, steam in his face, he felt again this impulse he gets to pour the clear glugging stream from the kettle onto the back of his hand, starting with the soft bit between thumb and forefinger, and then all up his arm too. This feeling that this is what he really needs to do, right now. He put down the kettle, clenched his fists to stop himself, closed his eyes and thumped himself on the side of the head. Then he made the tea. It was just a thought, really, he didn't think he'd ever actually do it, no more than he'd take his newest baby brother by the ankles and swing its tiny little fucking head against a brick fucking wall, which is another thought that pops up every now and then. It just, like, occurs to him.

He drank his tea, watched telly an hour, got dressed and fucked off out. He did go to the job centre, like his mum wanted. So he'd be able to lie and say he'd forgot, not bothered, when really he'd been there an hour, two. To see that look of disappointment on his mum's face. He went there, touching nothing, looking at nothing, talking to no one. He went and stood outside, smoking, acting as if he were waiting for someone, for something. After that … there was the library, but Violet'd not be there. It was a weekday; she'd still be at school. He didn't want to go not to see her. She'd be at school, sat at the front, putting her hand up with all the right answers. Writing in her exercise book, doing little circles instead of dots on top of the i's. But distracted, today, maybe, secretly thinking of him, of last night. She might do with his name what he'd at school seen other girls do to other boys' names: doodle it in her jotter, her textbooks. Violet 4 Ryan 4eva, or something. Covering it shyly with her hand, so no one'd see, but still writing it. He couldn't remember how these things went. Some such shit. He wandered streets, aimlessly.

When it was time he set out for Violet's school to catch her on the way out. He thought, vaguely, that it'd be good for her to get seen with a bloke. Maybe better if it were some bloke else, pretty much anybody else, but he was all she'd got. But then on the way he passed one of those army careers offices. Every time he went by that way lately he'd been eyeing it, the posters in the windows, the faces; this time, he found himself going in. That'd be next: get sent to Afghanistan, get blown up by a roadside bomb. Suicide bomber, even. Sitting there being talked at by the uniformed recruiting guy, the room slowly tipping, his brain's blood thickening, he could almost feel the edges, lines running jaggedly all through his body, a slight tingling, foreshadow of pain, the ragged edges of where he'd tear when he pressed the button, pulled the trigger, whatever, when he set the fucking thing off and blew himself all to pieces.

By the time he got out of there and to the school he was too late, the place was deserted, only a few detention-stragglers, and she'd never be one of them, not Violet. One girl vaguely familiar tried to smile at him, but he walked away before she could come close. He didn't like being at the school again. All he could remember of it was the fighting. Dozens of kids flowing out after the bell, coming to watch, hoping for blood. He remembered. He walked round the back of the science block, where there were no windows for teachers to see them from. He clenched his fists again as he saw himself hitting another kid in the face, and saw too Violet helping him, his imagination out of his control placing her there, viciously pulling Ryan's victim's hair from behind. Blood gushed from a split nose and lip, but it was his own nose too, blood filling his nostrils and the taste of it down Ryan's face. He remembered.

He came back to where he was. Where Violet wasn't anywhere. He'd grazed his knuckles punching the wall without realising it, white bits of skin scraping up like fraying, and he wondered if he was mad, where he could go to turn himself in. The army wouldn't have him with his head fucked like this. He leaned against the wall and squeezed his forehead in his hands till he thought it might creak and then all he could think to do was go get pissed.

*

He was standing alone in the pub, his lager getting warm in his hand, staring at one wall as the back of his head worked on making a dent in another, speaking to no one, no one taking any notice of him, when she spoke to him, the anti-Violet. A voice saying, 'Hiya, Ryan. Aren't you going to, like, drink that?'

He rotated his head against the wall, and with one rolled eye saw her. He didn't search his head for her name, just gazed at her leadenly.

'Stacey,' she told him. A shiny-haired girl dressed all glossily for a night out, short shimmery dress and makeup of the kind Violet'd never be seen in. Fake tan, high high heels.

Ryan eyed the swell of her breasts. He looked at his drink, his first, still untouched. The froth of its head melted away. How long had he even been here? But he managed to speak. 'Yeah,' he said. He tipped back his head and downed the pint.

'Blimey,' said Stacey. 'Did you need that or what?'

Ryan headed straight to the bar again. As he stood there Stacey's arm slipped itself under his. For a moment he could've mistook it for Violet's, and then he felt the difference.

'What're you having?' he asked.

'God, Ryan, but you do know you can do so much better than her, don't you?' she said, when he mentioned Violet, when she asked him if he was seeing anyone. He didn't know why he told the truth; because it didn't matter, maybe. 'I mean, seriously,' said Stacey. 'Violet? With you?'

He stared at her dully.

'I mean, just look at her. And look at me.'

'Me, me, me,' said Ryan.

'No, me.'

She posed for him, a hand on a hip, her other hand's nails drawing her skirt higher up one shiny thigh. His finished off whichever pint he'd got up to by then, and then let her take hold of his face in her hands, pull it to hers and drink from him a kiss. Fuck it. Only 'cause she knew about Violet was she interested, probably; meant to have him only so Violet couldn't. He remembered Violet's bit of advice on his snogging style, from only last night, best of his life, felt like ages ago now. Don't be so aggressive. Now with Stacey he first heeded the advice and then all at once ignored it. He held Stacey's upper arms and squeezed them so they must've hurt but she didn't wriggle. Lost in the kiss, his mind went blank, fiercely blank, and it only really comes back to the world when his mobile startles him, up on the church roof, later the same night, after he'd left Stacey sleeping in his bedroom, curled up and sucking her thumb. He sneaked out because he'd almost forgotten Uncle Dean's job, the church roof. Dean would've broken Ryan's legs if he hadn't turned up.

Pride in your work, Dean always says. They can't get fingerprints off lead, for some reason. Stillness. A fox screams from the woods, not that Ryan's any idea what it is – it could be anyone. The taut ropes creak as they ease down the next chunk of consecrated lead.

There's a sickening moment when his mobile briefly vibrates in his jeans before its ringtone kicks in. He scrambles to get it from his pocket before the noise happens, and so loosens his grip on the rope – it skitters and slaps its way down the church wall, lead plunges, some kind of bellow comes up from Dean's mate below. Ryan claws the phone out too quickly, it flicks itself up somehow, out of his fingers, falls – he grabs for it, misses, it bounces from the roof's guttering and goes arcing out over the churchyard, its lit screen twirling into the darkness as his ringtone spins off into the sleepy village night's stillness.

'Why you stupid little fuck,' says Dean.

A light comes on in the vicarage, then another. Shadows flicker across windows, voices. An oblong of light opens and someone's silhouette appears, pulling on a dressing gown and marching towards the church, shouting things. In the lighted kitchen behind him a woman's talking into the telephone. Two little girls' pale faces watch solemnly from their bedroom window.

Dean's mate below is limping for the van, Dean's own sweaty bulk just seems to evaporate from the roof somehow, he's down in the churchyard hurdling gravestones, shouting something about what a beautiful view, wouldn't have missed it. Ryan stays where he is. He'd seen a quick flash of the image lighting the mobile's screen: Violet, sleeping. He folds himself small into the church roof's crenellations, next to Dean's little heap of crushed beer cans, and hears the van speeding off. Dean's left behind, shouting at it to wait – he legs it instead through the woods behind the church. Soon afterwards a siren approaches. If Violet hears – and she won't – she might mistake the police for an ambulance, and offer up one of her little psychic wordless prayers. If she knew he was up here, maybe she'd pray for him anyway – but she wouldn't, because he's broken her heart, he thinks, like Stacy said.

'Do you love her or what?' Stacey'd asked, up in his bedroom, after the pub, lying back on his mattress. He was at the window, looking down at all the town's lights. He looked at Stacey, her naked body palely reflected in the dark glass.

'What, Violet?'

'Yes, Violet.'

'Yeah, we're in love.'

'And so you do know you'll really've broken her heart, yeah?' Stacey said, laughing. 'When she sees you and me, sees this – which she will – sees this in her head. It'll be all in bits, her heart.'

Broke her heart. He saw it an actual thing in his hand, red and bloody, a solid weight but delicate like the thinnest glass. With its own faint light. He crushed it easily, satisfyingly in his hands, and the crystalline little splinters pierced his skin, their two bloods mingling. As the pieces of it darkened and scattered to the floor he'd forgotten whose it was, his or hers, this heart broken. But fuck it, doesn't matter, break it, destroy it. Destroy love. How easy it is. You take it in your hands and just pull it apart. Only you don't know why. In a sudden frenzy you just rip it to pieces. Only you don't know why, hiding up in the crook of the roof between nave and chancel – words he'd know if he ever paid attention, to books, or Violet, or anything – listening faintly to the police talking below, wondering when they'll go and fetch a ladder to come up and inspect the damage, punching the ancient stone till his fist frays and bleeds.

BURNING MAN

ROWENA MACDONALD

'Excuse me, mate, d'you know the way to Eaton Square?' The man towering above me has the plummiest voice I've ever heard, looks like a stockbroker and is completely off his face. Everything about him is slurred. 'Eaton Square,' he repeats. 'What tube is it?'

'What?' The guy looks like the type that would usually tell me to get a proper job. I've been sitting between the east and west platforms for the past four hours. I've made about twenty-five quid and I just want to go back to Shit Street.

'What tube do I have to take to get to Eaton Square? … I've never gone there by tube before.' He looks at me as if only just noticing me properly. 'What the fuck happened to you, by the way?'

'Gulf War.'

'Oh.' The man is too trolleyed to react in the usual way. 'Nightmare. Look, can you help me? Some fucker nicked my wallet. I wanna get home and I can't deal with public transport.'

I pull my moneybag tight with my stumps. 'You want me to give you money?'

'Well, no, obviously not.' The bloke laughs. 'Tell you what, though: why don't you get a taxi back with me. You pay, then when we get back I'll write you a cheque. Actually there'll probably be some cash lying around, bound to be…how's that sound…?'

'Suppose you think I've got nothing better to do.'

The bloke frowns as he looks down at me. 'Er, well, if you've got some kind of appointment...'

'No, don't worry about it, mate. Let's go.'

Since the war I've had a devil-may-care attitude to life.

I should explain:

I am the burnt man. Yes, you've seen me. Sitting between the east and west platforms of the Central line at Tottenham Court Road. You've done the horrified double take, looked away again, all the while wanting to turn back to see if it's true. You may have even given me money. Kind people do. And drunk people. And guilty people. I don't know what they're guilty about. Maybe that they've got away without having to suffer like I have.

Actually I don't suffer. Not like you might think.

I have suffered. The burns, how I got them, was like no pain you could ever imagine. I was a squaddie. First tour of duty in Iraq during the Gulf War. A US A-10 dropped a cluster bomb on our tank. The diesel caught fire and I got sucked into the fireball, suffered 49% burns, lost my face and fingers. I should have died.

I've had 75 operations. They cobbled me into something resembling a human with grafts from my arse, my back and legs. Eventually I was no longer in physical pain but I wished I had died and I carried on wishing I had died for a long time. My life had been ruined by friendly fire.

'Yeah, some bloody peasant stole my wallet,' the guy is saying as he flags down a black cab on Oxford Street. 'Christ knows where. I've been in Mahiki all evening and I wouldn't have thought anyone in there would've stolen it...could've been the staff I suppose... anyway, god knows, I've gotta get back, cancel all the cards...total drag...'

The bloke is rambling: drunk but sharpened with coke, I reckon. I am watching the tottering, staggering, preening masses outside, and enjoying being sealed in the cab and transported away from them.

'How do you know I'm not going to rob you?' I ask.

This brings the guy up short. 'You won't, will you?'

I laugh. 'I'm not gonna rob you, mate. What's your name?'

He slumps. 'Brad. Brad Hamilton Sclater. Sclater with a c.'

'Eh?'

'S – C – L – A – T – E – R. Old Scottish name.'

'Oh right. A silent C….' I hold out my right stump. 'Lee Fitzgerald. Irish name. F – I – T – Z etcetera etcetera …'

Gingerly he takes my stump in his sweaty, white palm and shakes it.

'Pleased to meet you, Lee.' He nods at my stump. 'Does it hurt?'

'Not any more. Did when it happened, but not any more.'

'Bummer.'

'Yep.'

Immediately he loses interest, which is a relief, as I get sick of reciting the same old litany. Instead, he pulls a bag of white powder from his jacket pocket and glances furtively up at the driver's rear view mirror.

'Er, mate, reckon you should put that away,' I nod towards the cabbie who is probably going to run into the bus in front he's so busy peering at us. 'Not exactly private here, eh?'

Brad nods and shoves the bag back into his pocket. 'S'pose you're right. We'll have a toot when we get back to mine.'

'I don't do drugs.'

'Oh. Right.' Brad sweaty brow furrows. 'All the more for me then, eh?'

I haven't done drugs since 1999. One final blowout on the eve of the millennium for old times' sake and then I stopped. I realised I was getting fried on the inside as well as out. In 1994, when I first came to London, trance was at its peak and that's when I got into the scene. By that point they'd done all the operations they could to stop me hurting and though I could have had more plastic surgery to make my face more human, I didn't want to. When I lost my old face my old personality burned away with it and I no longer cared about anything. It was literally a baptism of fire. I'd been reborn.

When I came out of hospital I went back to the camp at Aldershot, where I'd been living with my girlfriend before. The army had given me a reasonable pay-off but it was hard living on at the camp when I no longer agreed with what my mates were doing. I didn't believe in the army. I didn't believe in war. I didn't believe in anything. It was very liberating.

I left my girlfriend, left the camp, and drifted to where so much human litter ends up. Soho. On the army stipend I rented a flat in Meard Street. Meard…mired…merde…I was literally living on Shit Street. Clever stuff like that I've only learned since I got burned.

I felt safe in Soho. It was good being an outsider among all the other outsiders—the tarts and the junkies, the trannies and the poofs. I couldn't work. Nobody would employ me: the way I looked would disturb people too much. Plus I didn't have any fingers.

So that's when I got into clubbing. They were nice the clubby crowd I got in with: as protective and tight-knit as my old squaddie mates. Only we were bound together by hedonism rather than war. Like me, they were a bunch of weirdoes. Strangely, a lot of them were into self-mutilation—tattoos and piercings; really pretty girls who'd turned themselves into a human colander the amount of holes they'd got all over their face. My all over scars were a badge of honour. Once they'd got over the shock of my appearance, my new mates were fascinated by my story. In one way I was untouchable but in another I was a touchstone. It's not just that humans are rubberneckers, wanting to peek at the freak. It's also that through me people can glimpse another world, another way of being.

I glimpsed other worlds through drugs. I could lose myself in music, in dancing, in Ecstasy. I could rule the world if only I could remember those amazing ideas I had at three in the morning, arms aloft, staring into the strobes. Eventually, ideas like that made me stop: I was getting too manic; I was going to drive myself nuts. Also the comedowns were bad. A few days later, the fear, the depression, it's come to this: I am a piece of toast living in Shit Street.

Brad's flat is at the top of one of those tall, white townhouses. To get to it we go up a lift like a brass cage. The flat is decked out in harsh industrial materials. Posh people often want to live like they're in a factory; I guess because they've never worked in one. The place is designed to look minimalist but Brad has destroyed that effect because he is clearly a complete slob. There are empty cans of beer everywhere; takeout cartons, their contents half-eaten and rotting. On the floor are puddles of magazines: some of them splayed open, some with bits of the covers ripped off to make roaches. DVDs: some in their cases, some out, some regular films, most porn. Sections of pneumatic, unlikely women catch my eye as I pick through the filth.

'Bit of a shithole,' states Brad. He slumps onto one of the two black leather settees. 'Dumped my girlfriend at the weekend. Been on a bit of a bender ever since.'

'Doesn't look like it's seen a woman's touch for a while.'

'The cleaner's been on holiday as well the last two weeks. Bitch. Gone back to Brazil, see her family. Amazed she can afford it: she's only a cleaner, after all.'

'Right.' The man is an arsehole and I want to get out of there. 'Talking of affording things, can I have my money back, mate?'

'Oh right. Yeah, yeah.' Brad heaves himself up. 'Yeah, siddown. I'll go and get it. Help yourself to a beer—loads in the fridge.' He gestures to the door on one side of the lounge. He's forgotten, or perhaps it's not even crossed his mind, that with my stumps it would be easier if he went and fetched me one himself.

The kitchen is messier than some of the bombed out buildings I saw in Basra. I nudge the fridge door open with my shoulder and take out a Stella between my two stumps. I crack open the can with my teeth and spit the ring pull into the sink.

When I return to the lounge, Brad has cleared a space among the detritus on the coffee table and is chopping out a line with a Sainsbury's Nectar card. Thirty quid in crisp tenners is sat on top of an empty pizza box.

'There you go.'

'Taxi was only fifteen quid.'

'Don't worry about it. You helped me out, so I'm paying you for your trouble.'

'I'm not one of your flunkies, mate.'

'Come on, stop being so chippy. Relax. I've got money, you look like you need it, so take it.' He stretches his mouth in an approximation of a smile. 'Why don't you stay and hang out for a bit? I like talking to you. You're a good listener.'

On the one hand the guy is a complete wanker but on the other he is all right. I manipulate the notes into my moneybag with my teeth—again, Brad doesn't think of helping me, which, in a way, is refreshing. I sink into the other settee and watch his surprisingly deft movements with the Nectar card.

'Actually, can I borrow one of those tenners a mo?'

He extracts one from my moneybag, rolls it into a neat tube and hoovers up the line. Gasping, he lets his head flop back.

'Want some?' He gestures towards the bag of powder.

I shake my head. 'I told you: I don't do drugs.'

'Oh yeah.' He tosses the tenner onto my lap.

'What happened with the girlfriend, then?'

'Fucking gold-digging bitch. Like all the rest...' And he proceeds to tell me in precise, manic and aggressive detail exactly how Courtney Anne, a Jewish American Princess, aged 23, whom he met in Chinawhite six months before, had done him over. In the meantime I learn he is 36 (although he has the heaviness and hair loss of a man ten years older) and that he is the illegitimate son of some big Scottish publishing tycoon and an American woman called Blythe. 'That's why I've got this godawful chavvy name.'

'You could always change it. 'It's not as chavvy as Lee, anyway.'

'No, I s'spose not.'

We both grin.

'So you sworn off women for a while?'

'Yeah...but I expect I'll get the urge for some action soon. What about you? Guess you don't see much action these days.'

His bluntness is shocking but, again, refreshing.

'You'd be surprised.'

You would.

I used to be a good-looking bloke. Tall, broad-shouldered, a prime physical specimen: classic cannon fodder. I've still got the height and the shoulders but the face is gone. First time I looked in the mirror after it happened, it was like a punch in the guts: I was a freak. Every time other people looked at me they would get that same gutshock. Every single time.

I thought my girlfriend would leave me instantly. But she came to the hospital every day and when I finally came home she looked after me, built me up. We even got into sex again. We had to be experimental seeing as I didn't have fingers any more but thankfully my tackle was still intact. She could deal with my burned face but what she couldn't deal with was how I'd changed inside. She wanted me to remain the burnt martyr forever and she the heroine for saving me.

I took a risky decision: I left her.

When I came to London, got in with the clubby crowd, I shagged a few of them. Amazing really. I wouldn't want to shag me but some of these girls were weird and experimental, and also open-minded and kind. Pity fucks I suppose they were. Or mercy fucks. Or maybe even nosy fucks.

'I just want to live a little bit of your story,' one girl told me, as she sat astride me.

'And the best way to do that is through my cock?'

'I guess.'

'Well, I suppose you wouldn't want to set yourself on fire.'

Now I occasionally have sex with Denise, a prostitute who lives on D'Arblay Street. I don't pay her. I would never pay for sex. I may beg but I haven't lost all self-respect. No, Denise is a friend. She's a high-class dominatrix but when she's escaped the whips and chains and removed her armour—the corset and the seven-inch spike-heeled boots—she's very sweet. We first met several years ago in Bar Bruno where both of us have breakfast every morning. And sometimes on a Sunday afternoon, when Soho is as soft and sleepy as it's ever going to be, she leads me to her boudoir and makes love to me and then we sit and drink Earl Grey tea. I suppose if I was a true mendicant, I would take a vow of celibacy as well as poverty but I've suffered enough: I need a few glimpses of pleasure.

'So, do you work?' I ask Brad. I've cracked open my second Stella and ordered a curry from a 'bloody decent little curry place in Pimlico' that Brad recommends. He refuses to order anything for himself and instead paces around the lounge telling me about himself. He's pretty boring as he barely lets me get a word in edgeways but I'm intrigued to get a glimpse of how the other half live, or at least how he lives.

'Work. Nah. I don't need to. Pa set me up with a bloody hefty trust fund.'

'Shouldn't go shouting that about. That's the kind of info that'll bring all the gold-diggers flocking.'

'Yeah, I suppose. But they're not gonna come flocking for any other reason, are they?'

'You're not that bad looking, Brad. Not as bad as me.'

He doesn't even laugh or seem to notice the compliment.

'Oh no, no, I know I'm pretty bloody good looking. I mean I'm not short, I've got good colouring. Courtney Anne used to say I had really nice eyes.'

Courtney Anne must have been either blind or lying: his eyes are small, piggy, red at the edges and have a mean glint in them. I am amazed that Brad can come out with such egocentric crap, especially in front of another bloke, and then I remember he is coked up and he doesn't see me as another bloke. I am just some poor, deformed sod whom he almost tripped over on the floor of Tottenham Court Road tube.

'What do you do all day if you don't work?' I ask.

There must be a tinge of aggression in my voice because he draws himself up and says, 'Well, I have various investments and so on that I have to oversee, I've got my fingers in a number of pies, a number of business ventures. I go to the gym…What do you do all day? Why haven't you got a job?'

'Oh, I regard begging as a job.'

I do. It all stems from Buddhism, which I got into roundabout the time I eased up on the drugs. Started going to meditation classes in a drop-in centre just off St Martin's Lane. I already felt pretty Zen; most of my future ambition and past pride having gone up in flames. I felt that what had happened had been sent to teach me that you shouldn't get too attached to your looks, your job, your material place in the world; that you could lose everything and still find peace. And I believed that through me other people could learn that too. But, like I said, I had to stop having too many of these extravagant thoughts. Like I learned in my meditation classes: you should let go of your ego.

I was running out of money by this point. Soho is expensive and the army's pay-off was big but not big enough to large it like I had been up till then. I'd got out of the way of work and of normal society so it didn't seem too much of a leap to sit down at the foot of the stairs at Tottenham Court Road tube and see what happened. I chose that spot because it was cold and raining and also I reckoned it would be safer than sitting on the street. Once, after I'd been out on a big one down near London Bridge, I'd run out of money so I couldn't get a taxi and ended up falling asleep in the doorway of a bank near Borough Market. When I woke up the next morning someone had left a packet of Pret sandwiches by my feet and there were a few coins scattered around. I was mortified but amazed at their kindness. I gave the sandwiches to a real beggar and bought myself a coffee with the money. Then I walked back to Soho, wondering how much you could make from begging and whether you would destroy all your self-respect if you did it.

A little later I was on the internet reading about Buddhism and I came across the concept of mendicants—people who take a vow of poverty for religious reasons and rely on charity to survive. You get them in all the major religions. In India people give alms to the Hindu mendicants in the hope that their holiness will rub off.

So I persuaded myself that begging was a valid contribution to society. My baptism of fire had forced me into humility and by begging I would be teaching the great shopping, consuming masses about compassion, about the terrible twists of fate.

You meet all sorts when you beg. Some are bastards: the pissed-up lads who tell you to fuck off; the women in chic suits who look at you as if you're a piece of shit that just got stuck to the bottom of their high heels; the tourists who whisper loudly about you and stare as if you're some kind of gruesome monument that ought to be listed in their guidebooks. Even the little kids who wail when they see you seem pretty awful. But then, among the lads there's always one who gives you a few quid and tells his mates to shut up, and there are the bleeding heart liberals who want to know whether you've got a bed for the night and enough to eat. Oddly, you get quite a few pretty girls talking to you too. Really pretty middle class girls. I guess they're a subset of the bleeding heart liberals but I think it's also because they genuinely want to know what it's like to live without physical beauty.

And then, of course, you meet people like Brad. Although actually I'd never met anyone like Brad before.

My vegetable biryani arrives. I gave up meat roundabout the same time as I started begging. While I tuck in, using my usual method of a spoon stuck into the sweatband on my wrist, Brad chops out another line. Sweat is pouring off his puffy face and his eyes have a skittish swivel to them.

'Mate, don't you think you've had enough?'

'Eh?'

He looks up at me. His bottom lip has a spoilt curl.

'Well, you know: it's nearly one in the morning. Tuesday night. I mean, maybe you should eat something. You can have my naan.'

Brad retracts his chin, retracts his whole body from the squalor on the coffee table. 'Excuse me, mate, but this is my flat and I can do what the hell I like in it and I'm not going to be told what I should or shouldn't do by a deformed beggar.'

I can feel anger rising. The blood I have trained to be calm through meditation begins to heat. I shouldn't have drunk anything. Like a true Buddhist I should have eschewed alcohol as I always intend to.

'I suppose that must be what I look like to you: a deformed beggar.'

'Well, er: yeah.'

My eyes burn from my burnt face. 'Well you know what you look like to me?'

'What?'

'A cliché.'

'What?'

'A cliché of a poor little rich boy. Holed up in your penthouse, squandering your trust fund on drugs, getting fat and ugly cos you're too lazy to eat anything but takeaways or do any exercise, unable to pull anything but gold-digging bitches because you haven't got the personality to find a decent girlfriend and nobody to talk to except a deformed beggar.'

We are both standing now, face to ugly face over the coffee table.

And then SMASH. I reel backwards from a blow to the chin and fall into the settee.

I haven't been hit since I was a soldier. Brad doesn't know how to punch but even so, he's fucking hurt me. I take five deep breaths with my eyes closed, nursing my jaw with my stumps. The old red cage closes around me.

I take five more deep breaths. The cage unlocks and disappears. I stand up and stagger to the door. I manage to unlatch it with my elbow and chin. Brad is gaping at me from the centre of his shitty lair. It's hard to tell whether he is shocked that he's just hit a poor defenceless beggar or shocked that I haven't hit him back with my poor defenceless stumps.

'By the way,' I toss over my shoulder. 'Shouldn't you ring your bank: sort out those stolen cards. Some peasant is probably going on a spree all over London right now.'

I let the door slam behind me, slide silently down to the ground floor in the golden lift and walk back to Soho in the soft of the night, my jaw aching in the cold air. I give the thirty quid Brad gave me to a bloke I know who sleeps in the doorway of Lloyds TSB on Oxford Street. And then I head to the safety of Shit Street.

So you see: I suffer, but not as much as you might think.

THE CAT

ADRIAN SLATCHER

I first became aware of the cat out of the corner of my eye. I was convinced that it had been there for a while, for though I did not think I had seen it before I wasn't entirely surprised.

There it was now, a tiny thing. It had short hair like a Persian, but its coat was scruffy as you'd expect of a stray. It had white socks and a touch of the same colour around its beard, but was otherwise a murky black. I had gone into my room to fetch something and it must have been sat on the bed for a few minutes. At first I didn't realise what it was, seemingly no more than a shadow, but then the shadow moved and I caught sight of the white paw attempting to untangle itself from a cotton thread hanging from one of the sheets.

'Hey,' I said out loud. The cat turned and for the first time I saw its face. It had such intelligent and knowing eyes. Then it was gone, skittish at my sudden appearance, or more accurately, like a guilty child when found somewhere it shouldn't be.

I thought there must be a window open and I checked throughout the flat but they were all closed. Who knew how long it had been skulking?

It had scrammed under my bed but even as I peered carefully into the dark underneath I suspected I wouldn't find it.

I let the bedroom window open as that was the only obvious

place it could have come in. Perhaps I'd absently opened it to let in some air, though I couldn't remember doing so. I did wonder how the cat had got in even from this direction, for though there was a rusted fire escape on the outside wall it was a death defying leap away. Nearer, but equally as implausible, a plastic water pipe finished just under the window.

After I'd seen the cat once I wondered if I would see it again. For a couple of nights I slept fitfully, every rattle or rustle interrupting my sleep and my dreams were troubled. The season was changing and after a cold snap that had wearied everyone we were overdue a balmy week. One morning, waking early with the sun streaming in through the windows (I'd left the curtains open after falling drunk-enly into bed the night before), there it was again, sat on the side of the bed looking at me, as if waiting for me to wake, as curious now as it had been scared before.

'How'd you get in?' I asked, only half seeing it without my glasses.

My sudden movement, as I grabbed for them, startled the cat and it leapt off the bed and darted away. I was just in time to see where it went this time, and if I wasn't mistaken, it had somehow slipped under the skirting board.

I leapt from the bed and zeroed in on the piece of skirting where I thought it had gone. My block of flats had been built in the 1950s and although I had been there some years I had always treated it as a temporary place to live and never investigated too much its fixtures and fittings. Inevitably there was a layer of dust on the top edge of the skirting which transferred to my finger as I went along looking for holes. I probed the wood for any breaks in the board or any knots in the wood, expecting to find a little 'mouse-hole' of some kind that I'd never previously been close enough to notice. I searched intently for about a quarter of an hour but found nothing that fit the bill. I could only surmise that the lip at the bottom of the board, a kind of curved bevel in the wood, could somehow be squeezed under by something small and flexible. My hand was too big though and could reach only so far under.

Once, many years ago, I'd been in a shared house where we'd noticed the telltale signs of a mouse infestation; little piles of sawdust on the landing and during the night a clawing below the floor-boards. Coming home one evening my housemate had isolated the mouse in one of the bedrooms and we went in together to trap it. What a superb foe that little mouse was. It gave us a merry dance, squeezing through the tightest of spots, escaping from us repeatedly, before, more by luck than anything, my housemate managed to trap it with a cardboard tube enabling us to carry the scared little thing out of the house and freeing it into the park.

The cat, though small, couldn't possibly be that much of a Houdini. My knees aching from the hard floor, I got up and reluctantly gave up on my search.

Over the next few weeks the cat appeared only occasionally and never as close as when I'd woke to find it looking at me on the bed that morning. It was if I'd been tested and found wanting. I would catch a brief flash of tail, or sometimes just feel that it was there in the corner of a room, watching me, but I was always too slow to react. I had an inkling that the cat was growing in size but I couldn't be sure.

During this period I had started seeing someone romantically. Most of this romancing had been in bars and restaurants and once or twice I stayed over at the house where she lived. Adept at the excuses and prevarications that men are so good at, I'd managed to avoid her coming over to my flat until she'd got an early morning flight with work, and with my flat being so near to the airport, I could deny her no longer.

I spent much of the week before she came over eradicating the worst excesses that accumulate unnoticed when a man lives on his own. Nothing if not comprehensive now that I was finally cleaning the flat, I was even running a wet towel over the tops of the skirting boards when I happened to glance up and saw the cat looking at me from a couple of feet away.

I swore under my breath.

'Meow,' it replied.

I reached over slowly so as not to startle it and for the first time the cat stayed where it was. I touched the tip of its head and it arched its neck slightly. I scratched under the chin, noticing that the white beard I'd seen previously was more pronounced. There was now no doubt about it either, the cat was growing.

It purred and emboldened by this I moved to pick it up, but this was too much for the cat and it darted away, though this time it at least stayed in sight. It was still watching me and as I reached over again I elicited another purr. This game might have gone on for a while, but then the doorbell went.

I'd lost track of time and my girlfriend was already here.

I let her in, kissed her on the cheek, apologised for 'the mess' and poured her a glass of wine. On some pretext I went back into the bedroom, but unsurprisingly the cat was gone.

During the night my girlfriend woke up a couple of times, her nose twitching as if she was allergic to something. When I drove her to the airport first thing in the morning, her face was noticeably red and blotchy but I didn't want to say anything.

'You've not got any pets you've not told me about?' she asked.

'No, of course not.'

'Then I don't know what it is, I'm allergic to cat hair.'

'No pets,' I said unsteadily.

'Well, something,' she said.

'Maybe it's some of the cleaning products,' I said lamely, 'I had a bit of a splurge before you came round.'

She didn't seem convinced and we drove the rest of the way to the airport in silence.

When she returned from her trip we met anywhere other than my place, and carried on for a few weeks, but when she split up with me, I have to say it wasn't unexpected. On my return to the flat I wasn't surprised to find the cat waiting for me, somehow bigger than ever.

'Just you and me then,' I said, and the cat purred in agreement before easing its way onto my lap for the first time.

Given that the cat had grown so well without me, I'm not sure at what point I began to feed it, but on trips to the supermarket it seemed the most natural thing in the world to put some sachets of rabbit or chicken or fish in my basket and on returning home to refresh the water in its bowl. It was usually untouched, but I couldn't be sure, so I carried on with it and carefully emptied the contents every couple of days.

I was busy at work and it was a time when two of us were competing for the same promotion so extra hours were necessary if I was going to impress. Coming home not knowing whether the cat would be there or not I began to get a sense that the cat turned up when I needed it, and other times, when I hadn't really the time to indulge it, stayed away. Whether or not it was eating what I gave it, the cat was still growing.

It had not been an easy year and I found myself becoming increasingly reluctant to go out, exhausted after a hectic day at the office. I would stay in most evenings, with the television on quietly in the background and the cat provided company of a sort. Then I got the news about the promotion. It had gone to my colleague. I was in a rage for days and it affected my work. I stayed out late, drank too much. I took a few days off sick and never quite went back. After a while the phone calls stopped.

I would leave the house when I had to, but it was remarkable how little it was necessary. A trip to the rubbish bins at the back of the house could be delayed endlessly as the bin bags piled up in the hallway, a stash of tins and ready meals was plenty when my energy levels were so low.

The cat was never the most sociable of animals but was happy to lie beside me on the sofa, or come and stretch out on the bed. It would only let itself be stroked with reluctance but I was happy to respect its space. Every now and then I was rewarded with an unexpected show of affection.

My days were increasingly a routine of prevarication, as I stopped in bed as long as was feasible, or lay on the sofa late at night flicking channels before finally falling asleep. I knew I wasn't well, but I didn't really think I was ill. My decline was a slow but steady one.

It is difficult to remember that time in any detail. Partly because of how monotonous the days had become but partly because of the weakness of my condition. At some point I must have become almost delusional. Waking from a long period of uneasy sleep, I began to panic. The curtains were closed and I did not know whether it was day or night. Stepping from the bed I collapsed on the floor. I was suddenly worried in a way that it had not occurred to me to be before. Luckily, some memory kicked in of the person I used to be and rather than remaining in this state I slowly put the remainder of my strength into what I had to do to get some help.

I managed to stand upright, and though dizzy, my eyes were still able to make out shapes in the darkness. I pulled myself over to the window and drew the curtains back. I wanted to let some air in but was too weak to unbolt the window. Instead I used the sill as a guide to lead me to the door. I staggered from one piece of furniture to another like a mountain climber grasping for a ledge tantalisingly out of reach and by this method I made it into the hall and a few feet from the front door.

In front of me, blocking my way, was the cat. It had grown even larger, or maybe its size was some sort of optical illusion, but either way its aggressive stance a warning for me to not to try and get past it. It snarled at me, and I knew I wouldn't be able to continue.

The next thing I remember is the hospital bed. The clean white walls. The tubes attached to my arms and my head. Time had ceased to have any kind of meaning. There were people around me who I knew and others - usually in hospital scrubs - that I didn't.

They tell me that I was in hospital for a fortnight before being moved to a recuperation ward. There I began to make real progress. The saline drip had been replaced with solid food that I slowly gained an appetite for and a session of physiotherapy everyday helped build up my strength. I didn't have many visitors, but those who came, visited often. They were friends who I had stopped seeing or work colleagues who I didn't realise were also friends. A couple of times, an uncle, my last surviving relative, came several hundred miles and stayed for a few days. Nobody really mentioned what had gone wrong, and everyone just seemed very happy that I was on the mend.

I hardly thought about my flat until a couple of days before I was due to return. I had the impression that someone had spent some time sorting everything out, but wasn't entirely sure.

They had asked me if there was anyone I could stay with, but I'd shook my head and told them that I was ready to go home.

The hospital car drew up outside and the orderly said he would come up with me to check I got in all right. It was a lovely spring day and the gardens outside the building were well tended with beds of daffodils giving it a light, hopeful look. When I'd moved in it had also been spring and this had been what first attracted me to the place. I had a single large rucksack with me in which were neatly folded the few clothes and effects that I'd had with me in the hospital. I noticed that most of them were new.

They had to change the locks after breaking in to find me and the new key was stiff in the lock, but after a few seconds the door opened.

The flat smelt better than it had for months. The bags that had junked up the hallway had gone, the floor was clean. The orderly made sure I was okay and then left me to it.

I opened the windows to let in a bit of fresh air, but in truth, it was less musty than it had been during my last few weeks in the place. I noticed a few little homely touches. A bowl of fruit on the table; a basket full of neatly pressed towels and sheets in the bedroom; milk and butter in the fridge. It looked like I'd just moved in. I looked all over the flat, in every cupboard and in every room. There was no sign of the cat. I noticed that his food and water bowl and litter tray were where I'd left them in the kitchen but that they had all been thoroughly washed.

As I sat down with my cup of tea the doorbell went. I was surprised, but got up to answer it. It was one of my neighbours, a pensioner from down the corridor called Miriam.

'I heard the door go, and just wanted to check you were okay.'

'Thanks, Miriam, I presume you've heard that I've been in hospital?'

She nodded.

'Would you like a cup of tea?' I asked. She assented and followed me into the flat.

We sat down.

'I'm so glad you're okay after what happened,' she said.

'I don't remember much, you know,' I said.

'Didn't they tell you? Well, it hardly matters. I didn't know what to do. I hoped it was the right thing, but I was worried and I called them you see; and that's when they found you. I think you must have fallen and knocked your head. I've no idea how long you'd been there. It gave me quite the shock.'

'I'm very grateful,' I said, and I was.

'Living on our own, we keep an eye out for each other,' she said.

We sat in silence for a couple of minutes drinking our tea.

'The thing is…' she started, 'it was the cat that alerted me that things were wrong.'

'The cat?'

'I could hear it all night, meowing plaintively, and when I came up to your door and knocked there was no answer, but I could hear it scratching. Two or three nights it went on, and I said to myself, I have to do something, I wasn't getting any sleep, you know? That's when I called them. I thought maybe you'd gone away and it had got locked in somehow.'

I looked at her intently, encouraging her to go on.

'Then when they got in, there was no cat to be found, and just you lying there, we didn't know for how long. I thought you were a goner, but they were brilliant, they got you in an ambulance as quick as anything. The funny thing was we looked in every room for the cat but couldn't find anything, it must have been somewhere else, my ears playing tricks, and just pure luck that I thought it was yours.' She paused and sipped her tea. 'I see the litter tray and the bowls in the kitchen, I'm not going mad, you do have a cat?'

'I used to,' I said. 'But I don't have one now.'

I walked into the kitchen, ostensibly to clear up the cups, but really I was just having one final check. I could be forgiven for thinking the cat had never been there at all. I didn't think it would be coming back.

Whilst I ran the water, I picked up the bowls and the litter tray and the remaining sachets of food from under the sink and put them in a carrier bag. Muriel was about to leave and I handed the bag over to her as she hovered, reluctant to go.

'Maybe you know someone else who could make use of these?' I said.

She nodded and took them from me.

SUICIDE BOMBER

MELANIE WHIPMAN

Tuesday morning and I've got a bomb in my pocket.

'Hurry up, Jen.'

I close the fridge door so slowly I can feel the magnet suck it shut.

'Jen.' Mum stabs her piping bag towards the clock, launches it at the sink and elbows on the taps. I slip my hands from the fridge to the thing in the pouch of my jacket pocket and curl my fingers around its fat fragility.

'I'm not leaving without you.'

She's been up since five, making about a hundred cupcakes for some toddler's party. They're all over the house, in varying shades of 'girl' - pinks and pastels, lilacs and lemons, all swirled and sparkled and scented. She started baking about a year after Dad died. Every spare second she had, trying to exorcise his ghost with rose water and vanilla essence, banish his memories in a puff of flour, icing sugar and glitter.

She sighs and wrings her hands in a Union Jack tea towel. 'Come on, Jen, we can walk down together.'

'Should have worn sandals.' She glances sideways at me as we stride along, 'Jesus, Jenny, you're wearing a jacket. You'll roast alive.'

It's been the hottest July for a decade, but they said on the news last night it's going to break. You can feel the change in the air, the thick soupiness of it clogs up your throat when you breathe in. Along our street the leaves are hanging from the plane trees like they've given up, and the grass verges are as dry and brown as old tobacco. The beat of my heart is loud in my ears, tick, tick, tick, tick.

We stop at the corner. Mum looks at me and I keep my hand in my pocket and stab my feet at the dust.

'See you tonight then.'

This is where our journey splits - she heads for the tube, I walk to school. When I was in year seven we used to hug here, a big rocking ten-second clinch. We'd count down: Ten, nine, eight, seven... Now I'm too old. She hoists up her bag again, 'Look, Jen, I was going to stay over at Mike's tonight, after I've delivered the cakes. You okay getting yourself supper?'

'Sure.' It's good that she's found someone else. That she's 'moving on.' I don't like him much; he's kind of creepy, in an earnest Louis Walsh way. All smarmy and do-goody and glass-half-full. Talks to me like he's my mate. Tells me Mum's 'on a journey.' That the baking's therapeutic. That the act of giving is healing.

'You still come first you know...'

'Mum. It's cool.' And I mean it. She needs someone now.

'How about you? You're not seeing Nat tonight, then?'

'No.'

My school's at the bottom of Kingstone Lane. It's a Roman road, so you can see the building from half a mile away, a pig-ugly 1960s' thing. Our sixth form's in the high rise bit, supposedly reflecting our status - top of the school. Some tarty designer put in these huge windows all round, not considering the cleaning budget and health and safety. Now they're splattered with pigeon shit and have been bolted down to prevent 'accidents.' I make myself walk faster, left, right, left, right, a soldier going into battle. A gladiator. Eyes forward, ignore the stuff flopping and churning in my stomach, keep my hands away from the thing in my jacket pocket. Past the trio of pine trees on the corner with their scattering of cones concentrate on the square of concrete looming up against the murky sky. This time yesterday it was bright blue, there were vapour-trail kisses high up in the ether, and I was still going out with Nat.

Now the sky's bruised a grubby yellow-grey, and you can smell the sulphur in the air. The weather people have got it right for once, there's a storm on the way.

I swing my arms harder and clench my teeth to stop them chattering. If it wasn't for Mrs Stevens I'd still be going out with Nat. I read some posh magazine at the dentist once. It had a list of the most eligible bachelors, with a glossy headshot and a paragraph of their assets - financial and personal. If you did our school, Nat Taylor would be number one. He's got the looks, he's in the 'A' team for footie, his Dad's a builder, so he's loaded, and he's as cool as you like. I've fancied him forever. He asked me out three weeks ago. I was in The King's Head with Lynn, sitting at one of those picnic benches. Nat pitched up with a couple of his mates. He stood so close to me I could see the little crosses in the fabric of his shirt. I imagined shifting my cheek sideways, laying my skin against the soft cotton. For a second I was terrified I might actually do it, and I wanted to stand up and create some space, but there's no way you can get out of those seats and look cool, not in a skirt. So I sat there trapped, staring up at him, while he stood there looking like something out of the Vampire Diaries with his black hair and white skin.

'Cigarette?'

I shook my head. His ciggie was cupped between his thumb and middle finger, and when he took it from his mouth, the filter stuck to his lower lip for a second, as if it didn't want to let go. There was this glow deep in my stomach, like someone had lit a fuse.

'D'you wanna come to Mambo's tomorrow?'

'Okay.'

And that was it, we were officially going out.

But not anymore.

Mrs Stevens is our English teacher. She came back last week after some mystery illness. I've always kind of liked her. She used to spend ages banging on about some random author or poet, but we didn't mind, somehow her passion sucked you in. I mean enthusiasm can be a real turn off, but with her it was contagious. She even managed to sell us Shakespeare. Daz and Scott Walker actually started laughing about Falstaff, I mean they weren't taking the piss, they actually found him funny. And she even got Phippsy into it, who's been off his head since his brother went to Afghanistan. She made it seem real, like it was stuff that could happen today; love and hate, politics and war. My very first essay, she gave me an 'A'. It was about Hamlet's faffing. I sneaked out a couple of plays from the library and took them home. I liked the way he tackled the dead dads, but it's the rhythm that creeps up on you. It got into my head, I started talking to Mum in iambic pentameters, even walking down the stairs in the same pattern, one leg then the other, der-dum, der-dum, der-dum, der-dum, der-dum.

But when Mrs Stevens came back last week she'd changed. 'Just write a poem,' she said. No pleasantries. Just get on and write. A 'free-writing session,' she called it. Suzie Crawford, the class swot, stuck up her mitt, her fat face all shiny with certainty, and asked what the 'theme' was. Mrs Stevens shook her head, 'No theme, write anything you like.'

It was a mistake, you need to give the idiots in our class something to focus on, everyone was arsing about, texting each other, and flicking spit-balls, and when she finally cleared her throat and asked us to 'share our poems,' there were no takers. No thanks Mrs Stevens, I've not finished Mrs Stevens, mine's no good Mrs Stevens. Every now and again her eyes would flick to me.

'David Turner, detention!'

'What've I done?'

She banged her palm on the table, 'Full detention. After school on Friday.' Her voice was all high and screechy and you could see this pink rash climbing up her throat.

Lynn leaned in towards me, 'She's gone loopy. Everyone's talking about it, she's given out eight detentions in one day, but they can't sack her cos she'll pull out the sick card.' Lynn stuffed her mouth against my hair, her breath all hot and huffy in my ear. 'She's had a mastectomy.'

'Shit.'

'You can hardly sack someone with one tit.' Lynn looked hopeful for a second, 'Maybe they'll have a full-out strike. No school for a week.'

When I looked at her again she seemed smaller and sort of lop-sided. She was wearing a loose cardigan, thin knit, with little pearly buttons down the centre that caught the light when she shifted in her chair. You could only glimpse the odd one because she had her elbows on the desk, and her hands clasped together under her chin. She used to be so cool, so in control. She'd never raise her voice, but she'd wrap us up in words. Words can be weapons, use them wisely, she used to say. She made us highlight it in our copies of Hamlet: Rapiers are afraid of goosequills.

I jogged Lynn's arm. 'I'm going to read mine out.'

Lynn drew her finger across her throat, 'Social suicide.'

'Ben, would you like to share yours?'

'No thanks.'

'Susan.'

'It's not finished.'

Lynn shoved her exercise book towards me. She'd drawn a pair of massive tits in the margin. I shunted it back. 'I'm going to read mine out.'

'Don't.' Lynn giggled, 'You'll make a right booby of yourself.' She cupped her own tits with both hands.

'Would you like to share it with us, girls?'

We shook our heads but Lynn was still shaking with laughter.

'Full detention, both of you, tomorrow night.'

'But Mrs Stevens, I can't, it's Friday, I'm going out.' Nat was taking me up to London. Straight from school. His brother had an interview and the three of us were going up in his car.

'You should have thought of that, Jenny, before you started mucking about. Full detention, tomorrow. I'll see you at 4.'

Then the bell went.

I don't see red. I've never understood that saying. For me it's like a giant hand is squeezing my guts. It's not all a bad feeling, there's a sense of liberation too, like you're so angry you don't give a toss about anything. I felt it then. The injustice. I was going to defend her. Save her. I used to have a reputation in my school for being hard. I used to lose my temper a lot. Dunno whether it's anything to do with Dad dying when I was six, maybe that's just an excuse.

But I used to fly off the handle a lot. Anyway, a dead dad and a shitty temper earns you respect. If I'd read my poem out, and spoken to a few of the other kids, I'd have sorted it, I reckon. They'd have laid off her.

After the lesson she was on break duty with Mr Gibbs, the tech teacher. We'd told everybody about the mastectomy, and we were hanging out with half the class, sitting on the field in the sun, making daisy chains and sucking the sap out of grass stalks.

'D'you reckon they cut out the whole thing?'

'D'you think she's got it in a jar?'

'A pound of flesh?'

I waved a half-chewed stem at Mrs Stevens and Mr Gibbs, 'You reckon they're shagging?'

'You're joking.'

'Dead serious. Look at them.'

'Never. She's only got one tit.'

'Maybe she's asking him to make her another one.' I said.

Everyone laughed.

'Out of wood. A Wooden Tit.'

'No sagging. Nice and pert.'

'Varnished or stained?'

'It'll be stained soon!' It's Simon, he's a pig.

She was right. Words can be a weapon.

I started it off yesterday. After my detention. After Nat went up to London with his brother without me, after he went clubbing in the West End, and after he told me how cool the 'London Scene' was. She was asking us if we had any questions about 'The Merchant of Venice'. I raised my hand, slow as you like. Her face lit up. 'Jenny, yes?'

She should have remembered her Hamlet, Revenge has no bounds.

'WOULDN'T IT be nicer if we went outside?'

'I'm sorry?'

I said it slower, with more emphasis, 'WOODEN TIT be nicer if we went outside. You let us last year. WOODEN TIT be better?'

'A nice idea Jenny, but I think it'll be cooler here in the classroom. Now did you want to ask anything about Portia's speech?'

'Mrs Stevens?'

'Yes, David?'

'WOODEN TIT be possible to look at act 3 again?'

'Well...'

'Mrs Stevens?'

'Yes, Scott?'

'WOODEN TIT...

I could hear the whole class whispering it, woodentit, woodentit, woodentit. The words spat and rattled like gunfire.

And her face went all strange, all still and flushed, and the heat bled down from her cheeks to her neck, to the top of her blouse in a big mottled stain. It was a loose, baggy blouse, with tiny birds and butterflies scattered all over it. Her hands flew to her collar and she held them there as if someone was going to rip it off. She was right about words. I felt a bit sick, my stomach swirling like the time I did cross-country and threw up alphabet spaghetti on my trainers.

Nat was waiting for me after school. He looked amazing, he must have skived off because he was in his jeans and T-shirt, and even though it was hot, he was wearing that leather jacket. And I was stuck in my crappy school uniform that I'd had on all day. He slipped his hand inside my waistband and tugged me towards him. When he kissed me, I could taste beer and cigarettes, and underneath it leather and sweat, and the spicy aftershave he wears. It was like I was inhaling him, layer by layer, and at the same time I was losing myself, dissolving on his tongue like one of those flying saucers Dad used to get me from the corner shop.

We went to the park again. I think I used to go there when I was small. I have this vague memory of being on the swing, an image of black shiny shoes paddling the sky, and Dad in front, with his arms out, waiting to catch me. But maybe I've just made it up. Sometimes I think I remember him, and then I find the picture in our album and I realise it's not a real memory, just a photograph.

Nat sat me on the roundabout and spun me round and round until I was dizzy. When I staggered off and pulled my hair away from my mouth, I could taste the metal on my skin, sour as blood. Nat laced his fingers through mine. He's got big hands - you can tell he's strong and sporty just by looking at those hands. There's a scar on his knuckles that glows white against his tan, when you kiss it you can feel the difference in texture, the scar tissue is all smooth against your tongue. He pulled me towards the bench and yanked me onto his lap.

'So what was London like?' I could see the Friday night girls, all skinny-hipped and skin-tight jeans, slinking and skanking on the dance floor. 'I wish I'd gone.'

'You should've come. Skipped detention.'

'I'll come next time.'

'Dunno if he's going again.' He put his hand on my lips, slipped his fingers into my mouth, then out and down, and under my blouse. He never talked much.

He unbuttoned my blouse, he was better at it than me, he did the whole lot one-handed - it's no mean feat, they're little buttons. And then he fiddled around behind my back and undid my bra and shunted it up, so it was sort of dangling under my neck in a weird lop-sided way. It made me think of a horse's nosebag. It didn't look very sexy. I didn't feel very sexy, and the whole dissolving thing had gone. He shoved up my skirt, and pushed me back on the bench. I couldn't stop thinking about my bag, which I'd dumped with my phone over by the seesaw; anyone could've nicked it. 'Nat. Wait a sec...'

He was all hot and huffy, and he was yanking at my knickers.

'Nat.'

'Shh... Come on Jen.'

'Nat!' I got my hands on his shoulders and tried to push him off. 'Not here, Nat.'

'Jenny?' The voice came out of nowhere.

'Shit.' Nat levered himself off, fumbled with his flies, ran his hands through his hair.

It was Mrs Stevens, standing there, still and small, between the slide and the seesaw. 'Are you okay, Jenny?'

Nat put his arm over my shoulders. 'We're good. Come on, Jen.'

But my legs didn't work.

'Jen. You coming or not?'

'I...'

'For fuck's sake. I'll see you later then.'

And I still couldn't move. He left me there. He said something under his breath. Something horrible, I think. Prick tease, maybe. But maybe I imagined it, because that's what I was kind of thinking. I watched him go, his jacket slung over his shoulder, his liquorice hair glinting in the afternoon sun.

He dumped me that night on Facebook.

Mum brought me up a cup of tea; I could hear the shuffle of those silly slippers I bought her for Christmas, and the clinking of the spoon against the china. She knocked on the door. 'Fancy a cuppa, love.' She left it on the floor outside with a custard cream. Mum's not one for words. She says actions speak louder.

Now I'm marching into battle. A suicide bomber. The storm's driven the seagulls inland, and they're wheeling over the school, squabbling and mewing, and strutting fat-bellied on the roof. They're always bigger than you expect, there's one on the school gates, watching me with its lizard eyes as I walk through. I'm into the playground, into the school, the double entrance doors swishing softly shut behind me, down the science corridor, and up three flights of stairs to the English Department, tapping iambic pentameters on the thing in my pocket. It's in time with my heart. Der-dum, der-dum, der-dum, der-dum, der-dum. English is first period. I sit in my usual place, wait for the rest of the class to filter in, chairs scraping, bags unzipping, snatches of laughter, comments about Big Brother and Facebook. No one tries to speak to me. There's a lot of loud whispering and I think I hear the words prick tease.

I'm all-alone, Lynn's not coming in today; she's got her driving test. I look around the room, at the posters on the wall. Hamlet and Yorick's skull, Ophelia floating peacefully amongst the reeds, King Lear clutching at his blind eyes, and some of the war poems we wrote last term. And then Mrs Stevens is here, clicking the door to behind her, face shuttered, scuttling to her desk, arms folded, cardigan wrapped around her. 'So, the Merchant of Venice.'

There's some sniggering, mutterings of a pound of flesh, and wooden tit, and I know they're ready to kill her.

I take a deep breath, shove my chair back and stand up. They all turn as I walk to the front. I'm looking straight ahead, but I can still see their faces, out of the corner of my eyes, like pale blurs, and I think of that poem we did by Ezra Pound, about people on the underground - petals on a black wet bough. My hand's trembling on the thing in my pocket, my heart's skittering and banging der-dum, der-dum, der-dum, der-dum.

'Jenny?'

Too late to change my mind now. I take it out of my pocket. 'This is for you.'

I peel away the paper and put it on her desk.

'Oh.' Her arms unfold and one hand reaches up to touch her mouth.

It sits there, pink and sparkly and sprinkled.

A cupcake.

'Thank you.' I say.

ADMINISTRATION: AN INTERN'S GUIDE

JOSHUA ALLEN

The internship started barely a week after my graduation. It was unpaid, of course; the class of naif that would complete a literature degree is expected to refuse compensation even if offered. In the unlikely case that my employer resolved to pay and had somehow learned my bank details, I would withdraw the money, fold the notes into origami lilies and arrange these around the employer's office.

While my friends' careers were launched at the Dictaphone Reprisal Units and Rolodex Internment Facilities, I happened upon a vacancy with Holistic Boom. The single, bold-typed word 'AD-MINISTRATION' filled the careers section of their website. Clicking on the link, I was treated to a person specification: 'We require a seething intern, who knows there is no 'I' in salary, to implode our nest of dust-busters. Must work well in sub-zero attitudes and be schizoid about logo integrity. Bitter knowledge of orbit translation and the ability to multi-task crumbs are essential. No experience is desirable, although full training is not provided.'

To help define some of these terms, a peer loaned me his business dictionary. It appeared that orbit translation was the most devolved aspect of logo integrity, itself being an ulterior motive of sub-zero attitudes, which merged into an occasional excuse for dust-busting. The crumbs could be ignored altogether, as they were purely hypothetical. I didn't keep a copy of my application, but whatever I said, they were sufficiently impressed to invite me to interview the following day.

Their email gave no address, only a series of directions such as If your shadow looks familiar, you're going the wrong way and Avoid the smell of freshly mown grass until you feel scared. In one aspect, it was wise that the interview time was flexible, as I couldn't be late; mostly it was awful, as I never knew when to abandon the task and go home. After an hour, I was desperate enough to approach pedestrians for help. An old woman answered me in a language composed entirely of vowels. Perhaps she had no tongue; I forgot to ask. When I approached a businessman, he rapped his cane on the pavement with an emphatic, 'Wholemeal bannisters! You call that brisket?' and walked on. I questioned a young mother in her pram and received only talc in the face. From behind the vehicle came a soprano voice, followed by the craned head of the daughter.

'I know Holistic Boom. I'm the Assistant Perjury Director,' said the child.

'Oh, marvellous. And where are the offices?'

'If you've got an interview, it's above the bull ring.'

'How did you know I have an interview?'

'Your shadow doesn't look very familiar.'

'Well, I suppose not. Thank you.'

'You're welcome.'

The bullring was a few streets away. It was faithful to the amphitheatre style, except the arches were now spanned by sheets of Emmental. Once the ring had been converted into an ant farm, the cheese's task was to dam the sandy loam inside. Soil was, however, prone to fall out of the apertures common to this type of cheese, expanding the ants' territory across the neighbourhood. On every corner, the air itched with the scrape of thoraxes and the tremors of tiny eggs. I crushed whole colonies to reach the bullring, though the more nimble of them leapt onto my ankles and advanced towards my petrified crotch. By the time I touched the first floor, my thighs held a phalanx of mandibles, and my frantic swatting didn't prevent several from raiding my scrotum. How the employees tolerated this every day, I couldn't imagine.

There were still two more flights of stairs, ending in a glass door.

'Holistic Boom, Inc.' was etched across it in a childish attempt at Gothic script, or a good imitation of a childish attempt at Gothic script; it was hard to say which. Before turning the handle, I noted that the door held two feet of water inside the office. I slunk past some windows, pretending not to look at the people who waded around the desks and photocopiers, but no drier entrance was in sight. Unsure of my next move, I returned to the door and knocked with an appropriate mix of courtesy and resolve. Some employees who stood around a whiteboard waved back. When I hesitated, one of them mimed opening the door, while the others beckoned to me through the glass. With a tug, the door swung open, and a chill stream passed my brogues and down the stairs. Swirling in the flow were spreadsheets, paper clips, staplers, some sandwiches, and a bouquet of origami banknotes. Applause erupted from all sides and then choked as a woman in a yellow suit strode into the room.

'Look at this,' she said, her neck cocked to one side. 'What in the fish-flap are you jackhammers clapping?' Some of the workers scratched their wrists; others stared fixedly ahead. I still held the door open, neither inside nor out.

Walking to the nearest employee, whose hands were frozen in mid-clap, she asked, 'You want the matadors back, is that it?'

'No, Miss Boom.'

She leaned back and laughed, her bosom throbbing like a faulty massage pillow. 'Well, I would,' she snorted. 'But then we've got a rabid bull lobby to deal with.'

The employee made a single nod.

'So who's been trepanning their uncle's monkey? Shit the pastrami, Castro.'

Without taking her eyes from Boom, the employee pointed straight at me.

'Oh, I see.' She paused, tapping a stiletto on the sodden carpet. 'And which mumbling thunder curd is that?'

'Here for the interview, Miss Boom,' said the employee.

'You're up the chutney fandango!' Her muscled frame squelched across the carpet, extending a green-nailed hand in my direction. Its touch was a bald arachnid on my shoulder as she whispered, 'You're a real dust-buster now, my pygmy groundnut.'

Before this could be elaborated upon, a series of tuned sneezes were piped through the Tannoy. The yellow-suited butch and her employees found their coats and started to file out of the office. I clutched at a straggler's suit, asking, 'Where are you going?'

'I don't know. I've only been here three years.'

'Oh. Well, I only just arrived.'

'Really?' The man, whose frosted eyes and buckteeth suggested a human strain of myxomatosis, grinned with excitement. He rummaged in the pocket of his suit and withdrew a matchbox, which rattled as I took it. He closed my fingers around the box and said, 'Have you seen my wife?'

We were now tramping down the ant-infested staircase. My colleague continued to gurn as I slipped open the matchbox and looked inside. It was packed with used matches; their heads had decayed into a black smut which now coated the inside of the box and the burnt sticks themselves. Quickly, I closed the box and returned it to him.

'Your wife isn't there.'

'What do you mean, my wife-' he cut himself short and glared. 'I didn't think she was in the box. That was a gift.' Again, he pushed the matchbox into my hand, more forcefully than the last time. 'Have you seen my wife?'

'Thank you, but no. I haven't seen her.'

'Is she blonde?'

'I don't know. I've never met her.'

'How would you know she's not blonde, then?'

'I wouldn't.'

'Right. So how tall is she?'

'I don't know!'

'Yes. That was always her trouble.' His gaze grew wistful, and his lips drooped over his jutting incisors. 'When I met her, she worked in the funfair at the Bank of England. Many clients tried to guess her height. Specialists were called in from all corners of the globe to help them. Later they called experts from the tangents and intersections of the globe, but they were useless, predictably. Anyway, that's beside the point. The guesses of all the specialists in the world were no more accurate than you would expect from pure chance. She showed them, all right.'

I watched the memory dim with my prompt, 'So what happened?'

'As a reward, she was promoted to funfair tour guide. It was just tiresome at first; for weeks, she was too tall to join clients on the rides, so she would narrate them from ground level. But one morning she appeared to be five foot six, so they let her on. Her real height was nine foot four. Going down the main drop, she was bisected at the breasts by a live cable.'

'Oh, I'm sorry.' I paused respectfully before continuing, 'So why would I have seen her?'

'Because she's your mother,' he growled, ripping the match-box from my hand and replacing it in his suit. At this moment we emerged into the sunlight, which slanted in the thick heat. The anthills were more numerous than they had been that morning; most of the tarmac was baked in a red, turbulent sea. A clean area remained from the stream of office water, but travel beyond this pale seemed impossible. Despite this situation, our colleagues were nowhere to be seen.

'Do you see them?' I asked.

He surveyed the street with slitted eyelids. 'Ants.'

'Yes, I know. I mean, have you seen our colleagues?'

'Our colleagues aren't here.'

'So where are they?'

'I don't know. I only just got here.'

I saw no use in pursuing this line of inquiry. While I formulated our escape, a fine trickle from the arch above became a surge of matter, dumping itself on the pavement and our heads. We scrubbed the dust from our faces, blew it from our nostrils and scratched the bugs from our hair. Unless something was done, we would join our colleagues in the silicate grave, which seemed likely as their final location. I dragged two wooden crates from a skip, gave one to the man beside me, and stood on the other. These would buy us some time.

Evening stained into night, while the sands accumulated under the lunar veil. My colleague was exhausted but remained on his crate, swaying somnolently above the tide. I feared we couldn't last much longer. The insects' level of organisation was disturbingly high, suggesting either external influence or a paradigm shift in the hive mind. It wasn't an effect of moonlight that formed the chitinous legions into phrases such as knick-knacks go home, hornswogglin' bumbaclot! and real chiggers 4 life.

Unexpectedly, my widowed colleague awoke and reached to me from his crate. 'Stop, listen!' he said, kneading my shoulders as if I had been asleep.

'What is it?'

'There's something I didn't tell you … about the ants. What is it?'

'I just asked you what it is.'

'How did I answer?'

'You said there's something you didn't tell me about the ants.'

'Yes … about the ants.' He looked down to where the colony was performing a ribald take on Caravaggio's Medusa, the snakes defiling the frozen anguish of her mouth singly and in groups. The image seemed to spur his memory, as he whispered, 'The ants pay our salaries. I think we've upset them.'

'No salary of mine,' I countered. 'I haven't signed a contract.'

After a stunned moment, he slapped his forehead in epiphany. 'That's it! They want you to sign.'

'Sign how?'

'With your name. Then you'll need a badge and catheter, but that's Boom's business.' Handing me an extendible stylus, he gestured to the sand at my feet. 'Wait for the dotted line.'

At his invitation, the ants formed a broken rectangle around our crates. The sand swallowed my mark as soon as the rod lifted, but it was signed nonetheless. I was expecting an end to the siege, now that a contract was in force. However, the first rule is to read the small print, while rules zero and minus one, respectively, are to read the medium and large print; on all these counts, I had failed. The message became alarmingly clear as the horde charged my crate en masse, crested its sides and plunged my lower extremities into an agony of itching. My main concern was for my head, so their halt around my waist was a small relief. I soon discovered that my preoccupation with the face was not shared by our six-legged friends. Like an electric current, they followed my path of least resistance: the anus. With the column of jaws rending my rectum, I gasped to my colleague, 'Is this the usual procedure?'

'I don't know, I never signed anything.'

'Lucky you.'

'There's no luck involved. Oaths are forbidden to me by God.'

'Can I be forbidden?'

'No. It's by predestination.'

Continued pressure from the rearguard thrust the invaders through metres of intestine, via the sphincter and into the hydrochloric hell of my stomach, which slaughtered the first wave instantly. But in a war of attrition, the ants' numbers would always triumph. While I struggled to digest the chitin of the vanguard, the second wave was mounting my oesophagus. A violent retch propelled them upwards, and a stream of squirming bile sprayed my brogues.

'Bloody fuck,' I gasped, wiping my lips with my sleeve. A strange hand brushed my nape, and I reeled to find Ms Boom standing close behind me.

'What an exotic phrase,' she purred. 'You must teach me sometime.'

'Can I ask you a question, Boom?'

'Anything, my surly diphthong.'

'All right. Why am I here?'

Visibly shocked, she stepped back and fell into the heaving sands. The ants, for variety's sake, formed a carpet beneath the supine Boom and conveyed her rapidly down the street and over the horizon.

'She was going to retire anyway,' my colleague confided.

'Can you answer my question?'

'Question?'

'Why am I here?'

'Answer.'

'Yes, I'd like an answer.'

'Question?'

'I've already asked you.'

'Answer.'

Faced with these evasions, the banks of my ire collapsed; I leapt onto the other crate and thrust him over. They encircled him on the sand, raising and lowering his body with greater and greater force until he was flung above the rooftops, his arc ending in a place unknown. Mid-flight, I heard a long, thin cry of, 'Question!'

I hunkered down, cradling my chin on my knees. The learning curve of the first day had been steep, mainly in a downward direction. I wondered if there would be a second day, or whether a taut wire would kill me as the funfair had killed my colleague's wife. But all was not lost; it occurred to me that there was one person, if that is the word, whom I hadn't questioned.

'Ants,' I asked, 'why am I here?'

The street flickered with grains of static. They seemed to be cogitating. Several half-formed phrases arose before the words dissolved completely. I had almost lost hope when, in the scrawling font which I'd seen on the door of Holistic Boom, they wrote the phrase You aren't.

'I'm not here, you think. Where am I then?'

You're there.

'Yes, but so are you.'

So what?

'I don't know, you tell me.'

You're there because I'm here. I'm there because you're here.

'It was better when you didn't answer.'

Exactly.

'That's very profound, I suppose.'

And that's meant to be superficial, I presume.

'Why are you torturing me?'

Nothing stirred in the breeze; in the crystal glow of the moon, I found no reply. Gradually, the ants vacated the street through doors and fences, leaving only dunes behind. By all accounts this looked like victory; but for what? I stepped from my crate and climbed upstairs, while a mercury vortex dragged my spirit deeper.

On reaching the office door, I stood incredulous. The water, the whiteboard, the employees' locations, in short everything I had once experienced, were there as before. Though my mind was raw as exposed guts, I reopened the door and dodged the items of the flood. The clapping routine, its interruption by Boom's entrance, and my identification as the interviewee were replayed. It was when Boom crossed the carpet that the cycle slipped. In place of the sensual whisper, she held a notebook.

'I need an induction report pre-shredded in my bin tomorrow evening. Leave the pasting to me. Cover from your application to the writing of the report, this dialogue included.'

I took the file, mindlessly eyeing the interface between her blouse and sinewed neck.

'Tomorrow evening, not last year! Schlep on it, Jiminy cripple.'

'Yes, Miss Boom.'

As I sat at my desk, a shiver ran through the plastic chair. The sensation was brief enough to qualify as imaginary. My attention returned to the report. At the top of the page, I wrote 'A Guide for Interns on Administration' and underlined the title. The second time, it couldn't have been imaginary; the chair certainly shook beneath me. Denial was tempting, and a lesser intern would have buried his duty. Instead, I leaned forward and found the chair's base to be surrounded by a platoon of ants. Expecting their imminent ascent, I clambered onto the seat in terror. They formed the words, in small type because of their limited numbers, Administration: A Guide for Interns. I couldn't abide this mockery of my work. Grabbing the notebook, I began the first paragraph, writing 'It was less than a week after my graduation that the internship started.' The ants, having somehow gleaned my sentence, replied with The internship started barely a week after my graduation. I was loathe to admit it, but their version was better. So was their title, so I borrowed that too. I hope, Miss Boom, that my honesty outweighs their collusion, as they have written the bulk of this report. Should you jump to hasty punishment, the ants would like to remind you that they pay not only my salary, but yours.

THE MURDER OF CROWS

MARC OWEN JONES

I knew just what was wrong. There had been no dawn chorus; no blackbirds anticipating the lifting of night, no pigeons squabbling, no crows cawing, no goldfinches, no chiffchaffs, no nightingales, no birds at all.

Earlier, in the dead of night I'd woken uneasy and afraid. I calmed my muscles and repeated a mantra of meditation, 'I am strong. I am in control. I can wish away restlessness.'

I had pulled my head down and withdrawn my arms into my nightie until my body was lost to the bedroom. I remembered that this was what I had always done, when I had been very young and very scared; too frightened to shout out, knowing that the terror was too close for Dad or Mum to reach me in time.

Light crept in through the gaps in the curtains and danced against the shadows.

Then I knew and everything changed.

When the house chatted into life, I padded through to the kitchen and caught my hip on the edge of the table. 'I thought you had a day off?' Mum asked with a hint of irritation.

'I couldn't sleep,' I replied and inched my way to the sink, rubbing my hip with my steering hand.

'Are you OK? You're not coming down with anything?' Dad sat at the table and by the sound of it had a mouthful of toast.

'She's fine,' Mum answered for me.

'The birds have gone,' I said to the window.

'Can you sort out the washing? Oh, and we need some milk. Another loaf wouldn't go amiss.' Mum sounded late and was juggling keys and coat, coffee and toast.

'What was that sweetheart?' Dad asked.

'The birds, they've gone, haven't you noticed?'

'Don't be daft,' Mum answered. 'Where are you today Peter?'

'Studio first thing and then over to the theatre. It's the first rehearsal with the orchestra.' I could tell he was excited, even though he tried not to sound it. 'What do you mean?'

'They've gone, Dad. Stick your head out of the window and listen.'

'I'm going to be late. Scarlet, don't forget the shopping and the washing.'

'I won't.'

'Bye,' Mum said and was out of the door before she heard our conjoined reply.

Dad pushed back his chair, its metal legs screeching on the tiles and joined me by the sink. He put one arm around my waist and stretched over to push the window further open. He breathed noisily through his nose and I hoped that it didn't sound as loud to him as it did to me. We remained together until our heartbeats matched.

'That's odd.' Dad stepped away and switched on the TV, flicking from one news channel to the next. Nothing. Nobody had noticed.

It was late into the afternoon, after I had finished all my chores and gone for a walk in the park, tip-tapping on the tarmac, my ears straining for any sound from the tops of trees, before the reports started. At first the tone was so light-hearted as to be inconsequential and I screamed at the radio, 'but where have they gone?'

Mum came home with a migraine and went straight to bed. Dad returned sounding tired. The rehearsal hadn't gone as well as he'd hoped and so I tried to instil lightness into the chatter of my wasted day.

Before bed we watched Newsnight. A professor of something from the University of Somewhere told the story of when Mao declared sparrows to be an enemy of the state. In 1958 he decided that sparrows were the reason for the failure of his agricultural programme and so he'd incentivised farmers to kill all they could find. With tens of millions of peasants following their leader's instruction, billions of birds were killed in a single season. And not just sparrows, the professor said, but birds of all species, heaped up in piles twenty feet high so that smiling officials had proof to send back to the Chairman.

The following year without their natural predators, grasshoppers were able to reproduce to the point where they blotted out the sky and blanketed the fields from one end of China to the other. The professor finished by saying that at least thirty million people died in the famine that followed.

The news the next day picked up on the interview and Professor Whatshisname became something of a celebrity. It was the end of the world as we knew it. I called in sick and listened to every broadcast, drowning in the repetitiveness, desperate for someone to explain, but nobody did. There was speculation about a global plague, a flight away from anticipated disaster, even an alien abduction, but all we really knew for certain was that the birds had gone.

People missed them, or appeared to, but in the way you miss a not very close relative who died a long time ago of old age. Wistfulness swept across the globe and people sighed in momentary regret before dismissing the thought and getting on with their day.

I couldn't go back to work and so I forced my supervisor to agree that it would be better if I resigned. Dad said he understood and Mum pretended to be furious, but she was too distracted to really care. The big news was that Nando's was shifting their menu to ribs and KFC was going out of business.

As the summer dragged by it became freakily hot. The smell of sweat hung over the City and the rats came; scampering through the alleyways, gnawing through walls, using the gaps between joists as their own private expressways. The noise drove me cuckoo crazy and so I spent as much time as I could out of the house. I walked through London, a cane's strike away from the curb and tried to filter sound by isolating frequencies, like Dad's sound desk at work. I turned off the familiar soundscape of life one frequency at a time, but as I twisted the penultimate dial there was nothing. Without birdsong everything felt false. Dad said it was like roast dinner without gravy, but for me it was like food without sustenance.

A dog rubbed against my leg and I jerked away out of reflex. 'I'm sorry, I'm allergic,' I apologised to the dog and the assumed owner beyond.

I stumbled onto the grass and was rubbing the touch away with my hand when I heard the song of a thrush floating on the breeze. It disappeared and for a moment I thought I'd imagined it. Then there it was again, a perfect pitch of birdsong trilling across grass, made sweeter through absence. I tripped over a leg in my rush to get closer.

'Christ's sake, look where you're going,' the leg spat. I held up my hand, ignored their apology and sank into the grass.

My skin simmered in the sun and I forgot everything. A chaffinch chased away the thrush. The perfume of flowers floated on the air, just out of reach. But as I relaxed a doubt jagged in my mind and it took several minutes for it to coalesce into thought. The song was too perfect, the cadence too pure, the variance in tone too mechanical, to be real. Tears washed the grit from my eyes and I sniffed so loudly that I heard people turn their heads to look. The song stopped and footsteps approached.

'Are you alright?' The voice was that of a man somewhere around my age; too deep and levelled with experience to be teenage, too light and lifted by hope to be swallowed by maturity.

'I'm fine,' I replied, wiping away the tears with the palms of my hands. I sat up, 'I thought the song was real.'

'I'm sorry.' The man touched my arm and it felt cool against my skin. 'I'm Simon.'

His right hand clasped mine in a handshake and I tightened my grip in response, aware that my palm was still damp. 'Scarlet.'

'What was wrong with my birdsong?' Simon asked.

'It was too good.' We still held hands, despite my arm dropping to rest on the thin chiffon dress covering my thigh. I didn't want to pull away. 'I remember birds bickering, always in a rush to interrupt each other as if what they were saying was so important they had to fight to make themselves heard.'

Simon laughed, a high-pitched haw-haw, like a magpie. 'Perhaps it was. I like to think they just gave up on us and flew off somewhere nice.'

His finger felt my pulse and sparked sensation up my arm.

'Except those in cages; those poor ones were trapped and unable to fly died of broken hearts.'

His touch was as gentle as a lullaby, electrifying the hair up my arm to the nape of my neck.

'I heard that the fires in Norfolk lasted a week. Millions of turkeys burnt, leaving behind only ashes and the stink of Sunday lunch.'

'Dad told me that a frozen turkey went for five grand on eBay.'

I felt the bones in his hand; straight lines to hard knuckles.

'There was one bloke, down in Devon, who'd bought fifty frozen chickens just as the birds left. He'd stocked up for a party and then thought he'd got it made. But word got out and three separate gangs came to rob the place. He died defending a freezer full of chickens.'

'That's why they left,' I said and he squeezed my hand in agreement. 'You should record your birdsong,' I suggested.

'I thought you said it wasn't good enough.'

'No, I said it was too good. You should, I think people need it.'

Our hands bridged the gap between our crossed legs.

'There are loads of recordings of birdsong. They've been clogging up the download charts for weeks. There's some ornithologist in Leeds who thinks he's won the lottery.' He let go of my hand. It was as though I'd lost a glove.

'But your songs would be new. My Dad can record them at home.'

'I don't think so,' Simon said in a voice that sounded final.

'Why not?'

'I don't know,' he replied with less determination. 'It all seems a bit mercenary to me.'

'You don't have to charge for them. We can put them on the net for free.' He didn't answer for several seconds, but slipped his hand back in mine.

'Ok,' he said eventually and laughed his magpie laugh again.

We held hands all the way home and he told me how he'd imitated birds as a child, pulling out the trick on high days and holidays. That he had just finished reading classics at Cambridge, but felt that he'd graduated into a different world.

I told him about Dad and how his latest play had folded before the opening night when the investors spooked. How Mum had become even more short-tempered, feeling as though she was the only person keeping the family afloat; which she was. I explained why working in a call centre now seemed so pointless. Simon squeezed my hand in agreement and said that loads of his friends felt like us.

He guided me the mile or so to Paddington in record time and it was only when we arrived that I felt a tinge of apprehension. It had been years since I'd last brought a boy home. 'We're on the top floor. There's a lift, but the stairs are quicker.'

'Come on then,' he said, forcing me up the stairs at a pace that I'd never tried before. Despite knowing the width of the treads, the height of each riser and the curve on each floor better than I knew the beat of my heart, I had always walked up the stairs at a measured and careful pace. But now we moved from a rapid walk to a jog and then into a run. I was scared and excited at the same time, floating on Simon's confidence, expecting to fall. On the top floor I pulled him down the corridor and we stopped in front of my flat giggling and out of breath.

I bent over slightly and put my hands on my knees, using this excuse to separate before opening the door.

Dad welcomed Simon like a friend, as I should have known and they were soon talking far more to each other than they were to me. I left quietly and went to make tea, leaving the door open to the sitting room so that I could hear them talk.

Dad asked an awful lot of questions: 'Where do you live? What do your parent's do? Have you got any brothers of sisters? Have you got a job? What are your hopes for the future?' I half expected him to ask 'and what are your intentions towards my daughter?' and I winced in sympathy for Simon. But he didn't and Simon answered each question with even-toned politeness: 'Notting Hill. Lawyers. No. No. I don't know.'

My stomach ached with pleasure.

They worked all afternoon and I sat on the sofa in the studio with my legs curled under me. I listened from a distance, their words like gentle breaking waves through an open window in the stillest of nights. They were debating whether a certain phrase was in semiquaver when the front door opened. Mum was home, so I slipped off the couch and out of the room without disturbing their concentration.

'Hi Mum.'

'Hello,' she replied and dropped her bags to the floor. She reached out and clasped me in a hug. Her lips burnt my cheek. 'It's too hot.' She went to sink and ran the water cold before filling up a glass.

'How was your day?' I asked.

'A few more pennies in the pension pot. How was yours?'

'I went to the park,' I said and as a quieter afterthought whispered 'I met Simon.' I heard her stop gulping and quickly added 'he's in the studio with Dad.'

I expected her to comment but instead she continued drinking, small regular gulps until the glass was empty.

'Are you alright?' I asked.

'I'm fine.' Her voice seemed resigned to much more than just the here and now.

'He sings birdsong. He's recording some now.'

'That nice, dear. Is he staying for supper?'

Even with the window open the night air clung like Clingfilm. We sat on my bed and held hands, talking into the dead air between us.

After the ease of the afternoon the evening had become more stilted and polite. When I had asked Simon to stay the night I had expected Mum to object, but she didn't and Dad remained silent, almost as shocked at Mum's disinterest as I was.

The conversation over dinner had moved onto a discussion about people who had lost their jobs because of the disappearance. Dad knew the keeper of birds of prey at London Zoo. He had resigned because the empty birdcages upset him too much and was now studying to become a blue badge guide.

We lay back on my bed and kicked off each other's shoes, our toes flexing on our heels.

Mum's heart hadn't been in it, but she mentioned that the manager of the garden centre had complained that fertilizer was going to become more expensive than gold. Dad was positive that bird shit was no longer used in garden compost. But we googled guano nevertheless and learnt about the 1856 Guano Island Act, bat caves and strip mining off the coast of Peru.

Simon blew cool air on my cheek and we cuddled, my back to his front, as close as two people can be with clothes on.

When my turn had come I told them about a story I'd heard on the radio. Some bloke called Stephen Pinkoff was suing the drugs company where he'd worked for unfair dismissal. His job had been to supply most of the six hundred million eggs that were used each year to germinate the flu virus. The interviewer had soon ignored Mr Pinkoff's personal plight and was more interested in whether the industry would be able to shift its method of production away from chickens, before the winter vaccines were needed.

I twisted my head and we kissed, creating a vacuum with our lips.

Simon had talked of a friend of the family who was a life-long plane spotter with a book that stretched back to primary school. He had left college and rejected a career that merited his qualifications to become the bird scarer at Heathrow. He'd employed the latest sonic canons and lasers, modified the landscape to encourage nesting in less dangerous parts of the airport and even kept a pair of trained falcons to disperse murmurations. Then, overnight, there was nothing left to scare.

Through the wall I heard Mum stifle her crying and I pulled Simon's arm around my body. We were both asleep before we could whisper goodnight.

Over the next week we stayed in and I felt every part of Simon's body to form a three dimensional sense of his being: his slightly crooked nose, broken playing rugby and re-set in a hurry by a doctor who was late for the opera; asymmetrical ears, flat against his head, the lobes smooth like freshly washed babies' skin; scars on his heel, thigh and stomach, the result of childhood scrapes and appendicitis; a dimple in the small of his back that puckered at the point of climax. I told him that he looked beautiful and he laughed.

In his turn he felt every inch of me with his fingertips and said I was perfect; from my mid-length hair that waved politely across my shoulders, down to my stubby toenails that caught on tights. He touched each small scar around my eyes and I told him of the pain of failed surgery. He asked me what I saw and I said nothing.

I didn't ever want to let him go and we lived in bed, naked, with the windows wide open waiting for the breeze that only came in the dead of night.

Then the riots started.

We heard voices punctuate the early evening. The sound of hatred intensified and sirens clashed into the night. Simon stretched his head out of the window and relayed the images, like still frames from history; of the build-up of people, some wearing balaclavas and others bare-chested with tattoos streaked with blood; of plumes of choking smoke smudged into the deepening gloom. A policeman went down, caught on the side of his head by a brick and so the uniforms retreated to be replaced by riot shields and batons. I sat on the bed with my arms clutched around my knees, grimly fascinated by the sounds of war and Simon's horrified commentary.

Mum rushed in. 'Get away from the window. They're smashing glass up the whole street.' I felt Simon's weight drop down and he put his arm around my shoulder. I let him help me to my feet and we covered our nakedness with dressing gowns. We sat down at the kitchen table and Dad made tea, letting Mum finish her telling of the night.

'It started in the bakery on Eastbourne Mews. You know the one, Slice of Cake or Slice of Life, something like that. Mrs Craddock from the newsagents was in there and said some kid had bought a cake, taken a bite out of it and then spat it out on the floor. He threw the rest of it in the owner's face and demanded his money back.'

'All cakes taste weird nowadays, it's the ground flax or soya they're using instead of eggs,' interrupted Dad.

'That's what the kid had said or at least words to that effect. Anyway, the owner's son was there and he picked up a baseball bat from behind the counter and laid into the kid.'

'Jesus,' Simon said, beating my reaction by an instant.

'The kid ran off, but came back ten minutes later with all his mates and smashed every pane of glass in the shop. Then someone started a fire and Mrs Craddock ran for her life.'

'It's the tip of the iceberg,' Dad said and he was right.

There were riots every night for the next week, varying in intensity from minor scuffles to all-out war. Everyone found a reason to protest, their legitimate concerns wrapped up in self-righteous anger. But I knew that what it all came back to was the birds; they were no longer there to soothe with an unexpected trill at the end of a horrid day. Instead birdsong had to be programmed into existence, invariably off Dad's YouTube channel, playing one of Simon's sequenced songs. It felt like comfort that had to be asked for, not freely given and therefore no comfort at all. I stayed in my room with Simon and interrupted fear by clutching at pleasure.

Then, as the heat wave broke and days of rain cleansed the streets, people snapped out of their lunacy and slowly drifted back to work. The urgency of radio presenters was replaced by light entertainment and Dad started talking about new projects. Simon cuddled up and whispered dreams of the future rather than thoughts of the present and past. It was as though the summer had never happened. I hoped that Simon would never leave and that the birds would return. Mum told me not to be so stupid, certain that they never would.

She still cried at night, but only after Dad's breathing had deepened into sleep.

It was Simon's birthday and I had spent all afternoon making a cake. I ground the flax seeds into a paste, destroying any texture that would betray its presence and beat in the flour, butter and sugar until my wrist hurt. I scrapped vanilla pods and melted chocolate. I baked it, counting off the minutes one second at a time and then tested it with my fingers before leaving on the side to cool.

'Something smells good.' Dad came up behind me and wrapped me in his arms. He smelt of smoke and wine.

'You stink.'

'Sorry. It was a lunchtime lock-in at the theatre bar. Everyone took it as an excuse to light up indoors. What are you baking?'

'Simon's birthday cake.'

'Oh crap, is that today?'

'Dad, I told you.'

'Don't worry; I've got a bottle of malt I can wrap up.'

'Just be quick, he was due home half an hour ago.' I felt around in the back of the drawer for candles and I heard Dad's clink of bottles end with 'aha'. I put the candles on the cake, placed it on the sideboard and when Dad came back in to the room, asked him to stand in front so that he would hide it on Simon's entrance.

The wind caught the edge of the newspaper and for the first time it didn't instantly remind me of the flutter of a bird's wing.

After thirty minutes and the fourth time of asking I let Dad join me at the table.

'He's never late.' I felt like crying.

Dad laughed, 'He's stuck in traffic, that's all.'

'I'm going to lie down.' I bumped into my room, crashed onto the bed and buried my head in the pillow. I didn't know what was making me so fearful. Dad was right, the traffic was back to its pre-disappearance worst and in all likelihood he was standing on a tube station platform playing 'kiss, marry, avoid' with the people walking past. But something was wrong. As everyone had pretended that everything was back to normal I had felt a pressure at the base of my skull and behind my eyes; a weight of indifference to the ordinary.

The doorbell rang, the pressure increased and I felt a pain stab my eardrums. I sank deeper and tried to ignore why the bell had rung against the expectation of welcome arrival.

'Mr Nightingale?' I squeezed the corners of the pillow against my ears and the voice muffled out of existence. I then saw, with the clarity of a dream, Simon standing on the tube platform in a trance, separate from the world around him. The delays had created deadened banks of stationary people, cheeks puffed out in exasperation; but Simon is serene, not feeling the digs in his ribs and the heels on his toes.

More people squeeze onto the platform and the front rank of passengers stumble closer, a white stick's length away from the edge. Further down the platform, a hundred touching shoulders beyond Simon, Mum closes her eyes. I feel the vice of her migraine ease and her shoulders slump.

The train's rumble stills the muttering. A wind rushes through the tunnel and out onto the platform. For a moment I lose Simon in the crowd, but then find him again, working hard to maintain serenity with the crowd at his back and the drop to the rails in front.

I'm back with Mum. Her pain has returned, distorting her vision into blindness. She sways for a moment before deliberately pitching forward. In free-fall the gasp of people rises to a scream, but only for an instant.

The policewoman sits Dad down and talks in a gentle voice. I know then that Mum had been the one who'd missed the birds most of all.

THE LAUNDRY KEY COMPLEX

AIDEN O'REILLY

I used to wear the same T-shirt and jeans for a week so it was a long time before I had to go down to the laundry room. I'd heard his name mentioned with a laugh, and the instant I saw him I knew. I watched him pegging out his clothes, one by one, with measured spaces, as though the maintenance of civilisation depended on doing it just so and no other way. I stared at this paradox, knowing right away this person didn't belong here, didn't belong anywhere. He closed the laundry door after him gently, to avoid disturbing the students who sat out along the corridor. Then he pocketed the key - that key which came to play such a pivotal role in his attempts to establish normal relationships. He stood before me, bulbous, six foot two, roundy soft muscles, an XXL T-shirt hanging off him like a sail. His long arms dangled below his waist. His predicament emanated from him like body heat.

'Hi there. I wanted to wash some clothes,' I said, 'so can I get the key when you're finished?' He appraised me cautiously, then revealed the key on the palm of his hand. 'I see. But you know I am obliged to hand the key back at the desk and not give it privately to another person. I don't want to cause confusion in the system.'

'That's fine, of course, no problem.'

He sighed, appeased. His fist closed over the key again. The battle scars of teenage acne were still visible on his face (but he had survived, he was there, still standing, grinning). Beads of sweat stood out on his nose. He was an acid test, to bring out the forgotten schoolboy self: were you the tormentor or the tormented? Didn't you too feel the urge to dismiss him, to curtly say: *You know what? Forget about it.*

But I didn't. My instincts were to distrust my instincts.

'I'd say you must be Simon then?' I said.

Simon hesitated, testing the tone of this question.

'Yes. That's me,' he said. 'How did you know?'

'When I was looking for the key everyone told me, check with Simon, he's sure to know. He's on the first floor. So when I saw you there, you seemed to look like a Simon.'

'Yes?' Doubtful again.

'In other words, I took a wild guess.' Simon laughed at last, swaying back on his heels. It was a laugh to see him laugh, students sitting in the corridor looked up at us.

'I'm Eugene,' I said.

'Eu-gene,' Simon said, placing equal stress on each syllable, 'Eugene', a relentlessly equal stress. 'I will leave in the key at half past seven, so you can pick it up. Please make sure you sign it out in your own name.'

It took a few weeks for Simon to become confident of the absence of hidden irony in the things I said, and of my respect for the rules of the key. He was not wary on account of my accent – he had grown up across six different countries in three continents, the connotations of my accent did not register with him. We had this much in common: we both had wasted half a decade after leaving school, and gained entry as mature students.

'Eugene. If you have no plans for Saturday evening perhaps you will call by for a cup of tea?' One hundred and twenty kilos poised in imploration. Afternoon tea, how delightful. I gave a quick nod.

'Fair enough, I'll drop by, sure there's nothing else happening.'

The dorm we lived in lacked a study room. With four students assigned to each apartment unit, the quietest place to be was often the corridor. Students brought out their cushions and coffee and lucky mascots. This block, for obscure reasons, housed an overwhelming majority of female students. They sat and read and smoked and read, the same book week after week.

I was a science major, and didn't believe in this kind of studying. For me, study meant laying out diagrams, working meticulously from the easy problems to the harder ones. How many times could someone read the same page anyway? And what was the point of all that highlighting?

I picked my way along an obstacle course of stretched legs, fearing a hip might swivel, my eyes might falter, and I would kick one of those shapely ankles. I knocked soundly on the door, one two three. *Just a moment*, Simon shouted. A sound of water gushing, sniffles, a long mysterious pause. The door eased open. Simon, grinning, huge. I caught the scent of animal hides and red soap.

'So this is where you live?' I took my time taking in the spice racks on the wall, the three pairs of polished black shoes poking out beneath a cupboard, a cardboard box festooned with customs labels. He showed me the pickles and dried chillies his parents mailed him from Indonesia, where they were now based.

A poster showing scenes from Kerry and Glendalough filled one wall. The colours had that saturated look postcards used to have until about 1986. Without asking, I knew that this poster had hung on his wall in some country where Ireland was a remote island of green shrouded in mist.

Because his parents lived abroad and this was his permanent home, he was allocated a three-person apartment to himself. Even so, the clutter crammed in from all sides. A shortwave radio, wicker throne, a huge German beer stein, a freestanding rack of shirts.

'Haben sie Sauerkraut in ihren Hosen?' I tried. Simon laughed, shook his head, no he didn't speak any German, though he'd lived there for three years. 'But for some time I went to French school and had to speak French when we lived in Gabon.'

Simon brought in two coffees – made with a real coffee machine, from coffee ground only minutes before – and I took out a tipsycake from my backpack.

'Eu-gene,' he said, 'this is very thoughtful of you. You know I thought about going out for some cake but there was a forecast of showers. If you prefer a sandwich I have some quality Parma ham.'

'Eu-gene,' he said, and I wished my fingernails would grow to points so I could curl them into my palms. 'Eu-gene, are you listening?' and he touched me on the arm. I looked him in the eyes, staring into earnest pupils until I should either hug him or punch him.

'Eugene, people in this country are becoming more and more materialistic. I have lived abroad for all my life until now. In other countries people don't think about money, and friends are more important.'

'Yes.'

'People are becoming more selfish in western society. Everything is centred on the me. It is an atomized society, people drifting from each other. You can see how there is little respect for the notion of community. This key to the laundry room for example. If one person gets it, they pass it on to their friends, and then it passes to someone else, and the register at the desk is useless, it has lost any connection to reality. I looked for the key once and was told that Lysaght had it in room 408. I went there and she no longer had it. But please, I said, you are responsible for the key, can I ask you to get it for me. And she looked at me,' he whisked his fingers, 'like I was nothing, not a person worthy to speak to. Not even a person at all. I went to the room number she told me, and some woman there, slightly older-looking, maybe a post-doc, she said she was not yet finished. I said that's fine, I understand, I will come back later. But please, can you sign your name on the register downstairs so other people will know where the key is. And she looked at me like I was a hippopotamus. I said to her, it is important to have a system. Please, do this for the benefit of everybody. And she threw the key at me and slammed the door. I stood there in shock. Can you believe this? Then I heard a mumbling behind the door so I stood closer to listen. I was wondering, what is this noise? She was praying to God, saying please help me God, make him go away. Maybe she could see me through a crack. I was still standing there because I was in total shock. This is something extraordinary Eugene. Do I -' and here he shrugged with his whole arms, 'do I look like a monster?'

I laughed breathlessly, sprang up from the couch and grabbed a book at random. *St. Andrew's, Nairobi* was rubber-stamped on the inside cover. I thumbed my way along the shelf. Several pulpy schoolbooks in French, a volume entitled *Coming to Terms with Yourself*, a book of Yoruba mythology. The shelves told of a childhood spread across Africa, Germany, and Singapore. As a kid he must have played with black kids in Nairobi, clapped hands to Christian chants. Or maybe bummed on a beach with the international jet set. Where were the traces of that in him? Where did he get himself from?

'Please Eugene, why do you walk around so much?'

I flopped back into the armchair again. 'You do psychology? You have all the books up there...'

Simon took off his glasses and rubbed his eyes. This constant rubbing didn't redden them, rather there was a bruised yellow pallor around the eyelids.

'There is something I wanted to tell you Eugene.'

Yes, but why can you not just tell it? Why this feeling of suffocation, a leaning forward, eye contact?

Simon waited intransigently for my nod of assent. Then the terrible intimacy emerged.

'I visit a psychoanalyst.'

'Oh.'

'I am following a series of therapy sessions.'

This was a moment unshackled from the ordinary. I did not want to say anything silly or ironic. 'What is he trying to cure?'

'It's a developmental problem.' He hesitated, but not from embarrassment. 'A problem of excessive self-image. I need to overcome a barrier before I can establish normal relations with people.'

'And what is this barrier?'

'I can't tell you everything, it might interfere with the treatment. But what I need to achieve is the ability to cope with normal situations. There is a pragmatics of everyday life that I need to master. The aim is not to become normal...' Simon frowned. 'But to be aware of the normal and have it as an option.'

'I see.'

'My problem is not a psychological illness as such. The root problem - though problem is not the right word, it's more a facet of my personality - is a feeling of superiority.'

The breath stopped in my throat and wavered. I could not believe that humans could speak like this. Words were not used like this where I came from. My parents always spoke like they were in a sworn pact to never say a thing beyond the grindingly mundane.

'This is not a fully conscious feeling,' Simon continued. 'I am not walking around thinking the world should worship me. I don't believe what this complex is telling me, it's just a little subconscious part of me. With the analyst's help we are dragging it into the daylight. Now I am more relaxed about chatting with ordinary people. I know each conversation does not have to be full of meaning. It can be little pointless things just to be friendly. I have learned to isolate this inner self and cut it off, saying no, you are trying to delude me. In this way I can relax. I do voluntary work with the Cyril Park restoration team. We have great fun, we plant rose beds and lay out cobble paths. We're applying for real cobbles – there's a big stock of them held by the city council. And we make sandwiches and share them out between us, and we have a cheese and wine party at the end of the month and have fun … but to be truthful, Eugene - maybe I do think a little more deeply than other people.'

I avoided the laundry room after that. I stayed clear of the first floor altogether. There was nowhere left for a conversation to go now it had turned a spotlight around on itself. *Let's talk about being friends Simon, let's talk about how well we can talk about simple things.*

I brought my bags of clothes to a launderette in town instead. The machine was great at washing the clothes, but not so great at drying them. That was the big advantage of the dorm laundry room. It had special radiators under the lines to dry clothes thoroughly. When I hung them in my room they made the air damp and I woke up sweaty.

I was playing poker one night in Hamilton block with a group of students. One of them, a guy called Carnew, used to stare his opponent in the eyes and say *I know you think I know what you're thinking*. It turned out he was a psychology student. I dropped the name Simon to him, but without implying I was a friend. He started laughing.

'Simon, Simon,' he said, 'gets into endless debates with the lec-
turers about the foundations of psychology, wanting to go right
back to the ego – id differentiation and restructure it.'

'He knows his stuff then?'

'Not at all. He always gets crappy marks for his essays. And the
funny thing is, he never lets it bother him. He still keeps talking
and talking like he's an expert. He gets the library staff to order
specialised books for him. I didn't know you could request books
from the library, but if you look as if you know what you're doing,
you can.'

It was mid-term break that weekend. I went back to my home
area. For ten days I was renovating the parents' kitchen by day and
boozing with old schoolfriends by night. We had a good laugh
at how the ones the old CB teachers had labelled dunces were
now doing pretty well for themselves. Phil was running a restaurant
employing three Poles, Mark was selling thirty cars a week at five
percent commission. They were all proud of being down-to-earth.
All with an expert ease of knowing exactly when and with what
emphasis to declare *bullshit*.

I was sitting outside the Lincoln lecture hall when I heard Simon's
unmistakable pronunciation of my name. He greeted me with no
hint of shame or awkwardness. We went for a coffee. He chatted
about the recent spell of bad weather, the changed opening hours
of the library, and a Louise Brooks season the film club was showing that week. He gave a wry smile as he left, as though to acknowledge this successful exercise in making small talk. I promised to
call by some time soon.

'You can visit him too,' he whispered. The odour of decadence is a
blend of shoe polish and burnt coffee. Its sound is a heavy breath
being exhaled. 'I mentioned you to him and he said it was possible.'

I gave a small nod of assent.

'He doesn't charge a fixed fee, just pay what you can afford. And
please, don't think in terms of what problem you have. He won't
even ask you if you have a problem, he won't ask why you are
there. Think of it as a journey inwards. And Eugene. You will not

feel better afterwards. '

'Going to visit turnip-head again? How can you stand him?' Eyes shining with derision. She was one of the girls who sit out in the corridor.

'I know, he's a terror,' I answered easily, hunkering down, because she was the kind of girl any guy would stop to talk to if given half a chance.

'Old Mushroom we call him,' she said. That was exactly how I pictured Simon too: a fantastic growth in a neglected nook of the house, the diametrical opposite of a flower in the sun.

'Old Mushroom?' I laughed. 'A minute ago he was a turnip. He must be the whole vegetable soup.'

'Why do you go visit him?' She seemed to take it as a personal affront.

'He has good coffee, real stuff his parents post over from Indonesia.'

'You'd sit with a weirdo for *five* hours just to get a really good cup of coffee?'

We set off to the psychoanalyst, big friend Simon and I, strolling the gauntlet of a dozen sprawled female legs, grinning defiantly.

And when we got to the shabby waiting room, a half-dozen assorted souls were sitting, young and old, not ashamed to acknowledge that we are not as simple as we would wish. Who had all escaped from the insistent *I am what I am*. And I understood that even those who seem the most uncomplicated, the bar stool tenants, the flag wavers who have never read a book in their lives, even my own parents too, were all constantly circling a vortex of thought, and shied away from it with all the strength of their healthy instincts.

Now the psychoanalyst, our Charon, emerged. A mild man in appearance, with greying sideburns and a lozenge-patterned jumper.

'Next,' he said in a tired voice. And I felt the old childish tremor within me, the thought of a secret divine spark, my hidden hero self, and that it might be revealed and might shine.

THE ANGEL

SARAH EVANS

Davie kept babbling about angels. 'In the garden,' he said. 'Under the water.'

'Perhaps a water nymph,' Michael said, wondering what fairy stories the child had been told.

'An angel,' Davie insisted. 'Like on the Christmas tree. All icicle-y.' He shifted his warm little body away and burrowed further down beneath the duvet.

'Sweet dreams,' Michael said and leant across to press his lips against the powdery softness of his son's cheek; a small fist emerged to rub the kiss off. Michael stayed a moment, breathing in the minty sweetness of the boy, watching as he drifted instantly into slumber. What did four-year-olds dream about?

Angels, perhaps.

*

Downstairs, he went into the living room and looked up at the top of the tree. Angel or fairy? He was damned if he could tell the difference. The ornament was carved from pale wood and clothed in frothy white. Some sort of tiara or halo glittered round the head and wings in spiky lace sprouted improbably from somewhere at the back. Ciara would have chosen the thing with disproportionate care – one of those artisan Christmas fairs that she knew better than to drag him to. His own family had never taken Christmas seriously and Ciara's insistence on rituals and endless paraphernalia jarred.

He found Ciara in the kitchen, bending down to open the oven, releasing a waft of cinnamon-scented warmth. She placed the baking tray on the side. The mince pies were golden brown and the tar-like filling bubbled out from the criss-crosses placed in each centre.

'They smell good,' he said, knowing that he'd find them sickly but he ought to show appreciation when she'd made the effort.

'For the Church Carol Service,' she said.

'Ah.'

'But I can keep some. If you like.'

'Yes.'

'Though I didn't think you liked them.'

'I like yours.'

Her smile failed to reach her eyes.

The two of them seemed reduced to polite exchanges. At least they were being polite; better than the arguments of recent months, which seemed to blister up out of nowhere before pricking to nothingness leaving him barely able to remember the cause.

'Davie keeps going on about angels in the garden.'

'Yes.'

'You know what it's about?'

'He's four years old. It's Christmas. Of course he thinks there are angels everywhere.'

He wondered what Ciara had been telling Davie. He'd consented – reluctantly – to talk about Father Christmas as if he were real, and he expected Ciara to also keep to what they had agreed, that theirs would be a secular household. Davie would make up his own mind when he came to be an adult, but Michael wasn't having any child of his indoctrinated in biblical myths.

When they met, Ciara had regaled him with stories from her convent school, the puritanical, prurient attitudes to sex from black-veiled nuns, which provoked hilarity amongst teenage girls. She had never quite abandoned the ceremony, the Christmas carols and so on. Only recently had she started going regularly to the nearby church, claiming that actually there was more to her church going than the sing-along in beautiful surrounds; only recently had she used words like faith.

'What's for dinner?' he asked.

'Whatever you want.' She held up her hands. 'As you can see I've been baking so I haven't had time to cook your dinner and I don't need anything given I'm going out.'

'Out?' She'd been out a lot recently. His work had been busy and he arrived home too drained of energy to do anything other than flop in front of the TV.

'I did tell you.'

She often claimed he didn't remember the things she said. He didn't see that the lapses of memory were necessarily his, but he'd promised himself not to engage in petty disputes, not over Christmas.

*

The house was quiet after Ciara left, and cold. Building a fire seemed too much effort just for him. He thought about ringing for takeaway, but with the fridge and every cupboard bursting with food it felt profligate. Rummaging through cans of custard, white sauce, butter beans, half-used packets of this and that, he found supermarket-basics baked beans. Ciara knew he preferred Heinz. But he was the only one to eat beans on toast and she couldn't be expected to remember all his faddy preferences. He could hear her telling him that. Two mince pies dusted in a light snowfall of icing sugar were left out on a plate. Was he supposed to eat both, or leave one for her?

The beans were bubbling, but the toast needed a minute longer. Outside, the moon was bright and the twisted, overgrown trees glittered in its glow. Ciara and he had loved the house when they bought it, its rambling size, the untamed garden with reed-framed pond attracting frogs and ducks and herons. They'd been drawn to its isolation, offering peace and quiet. He'd wondered recently if it hadn't served to cut them off from the ebb and flow of other people, pushing them too much onto themselves.

The frozen surface of the pond shimmered twenty yards away.

Davie was old enough to understand how he absolutely must not step out onto its frozen surface, but all this talk of waterlogged angels reminded Michael that he ought to talk to Davie again. You couldn't repeat these things too often.

He caught the scent of burning toast.

*

It wasn't until the next day that he discovered the body.

He woke early, his mind anticipating the alarm clock that usually trilled him into the day. On Christmas Eve, he could allow himself a lie in, but once awake he felt restless. Ciara was asleep. She had come back late; quite how late, he didn't know. She hadn't been back when he headed for bed at sometime after eleven. Nor had she been in bed at half past midnight when something in the house had creaked and woken him. But now it was seven-thirty and she was solidly asleep beside him.

He eased himself slowly from beneath the covers, not wanting to disturb her, not wanting to feel obliged to offer to bring coffee back to bed. Standing in the kitchen, he felt overcome with weariness, perverse when moments ago his body had urged him to get up. The sun was only just rising, casting a reddish glow over the frosted trees. He thought he saw something.

He rubbed his eyes and looked again, seeing nothing but the winter scene. He was just tired, that was all.

The kettle boiled and he heaped coffee granules into his tannin-stained college mug. He added milk and burned his lips on the first bitter mouthful. His eye seemed to catch on something again, but then discovered nothing when he actually focussed. He pulled his dressing gown tighter and replaced his slippers with the worn out trainers he used for gardening, opened the back door, and plunged forward, clamping his jaw against the chill.

Snow crunched beneath his feet; his toes instantly began to freeze; his breath misted in the air and his eyes failed to make sense of what it was that they were seeing. His heart pounded. It couldn't be; this absolutely could not be real.

He could see distinctly now, but he continued right up until his toes cracked the icy edges of the pond. Beneath the layer of blue ice lay the body of a girl. She was face down and wearing some kind of full-skirted dress that spread around her. Her hair formed a frozen halo.

An angel.

*

To be standing in his own hallway dialling 999 felt surreal. Should he alert Ciara first? He nearly put the phone down but already someone was asking which of the emergency services he required.

'Ambulance,' he said. Far too late for that. 'And police.' Pressing to disconnect the call, he wondered if he could have imagined the thing, whether Davie's childish fancies had infected him. He started, filled with an intense and unnamed fear, as he sensed a presence behind him.

'Michael!' Ciara said quite sharply and he wondered what she had glimpsed on his face. 'Who are you ringing?'

His hand was still clutching the phone, the knuckles white and shiny. Repeating his story to Ciara, he felt more and more certain that he must have been mistaken; he must be going insane. Her tightly pressed lips seemed to confirm she thought that too.

'You're sure?' she asked.

'Sure enough to ring the police.'

'It's not the light playing tricks?'

'Well I didn't think so. Or I wouldn't have dialled 999.' Obviously.

He wished she would simply believe him; he longed for the Ciara he used to know, the one who would have accepted his word unquestioningly, who would have come close to wrap her warmth around him.

'I'd better look.'

He watched as she re-enacted his earlier movements, tugging her dressing gown close, seeking outdoor shoes, heading out. He thought of that other Michael who would have accompanied her, rather than letting her face what was out there alone.

She stayed only a second or two by the pond. When she returned her face was blue-white. 'Well clearly there's something there,' she said. 'Maybe it's a shop-mannequin or something.'

He waited to feel the relief provided by her explanation. Those smooth contours of a female form, the spread of fabric and hair, could she be right, they were plastic and nothing more? His stomach refused to unclench from its conviction.

A girl's body lay frozen in their pond.

*

Time passed oddly. He waited in slow-motion limbo for the sound of sirens and vehicles up their pot-holed drive. Around him, Ciara flurried. She didn't want Davie here when the police arrived. Michael nodded, not wanting, not really, to deal with this on his own, but failing to protest. Just as he didn't say that perhaps she should be here, and Davie too, as witnesses. Or ask why, if it was a shop-dummy, it mattered.

'Isn't Daddy coming?' Davie asked, his blue eyes wide above the colourful scarf which Ciara coiled round his neck.

'Not today,' Ciara said. 'Just you and me going out for breakfast. Isn't that fun?'

Davie looked worried; it was a mistake to use words like fun when it would be obvious even to a four-year-old that fun did not come into it.

Michael propped himself against the window to see if the family car would encounter emergency-service vehicles coming the other way along the narrow lane. He waited and there was no sound to interrupt the absolute stillness that had so attracted them to the house. He settled into his vigil. Pointless to pretend he could settle to anything else.

Time slowed further, grinding to a virtual stop. Perhaps no one was coming, his call dismissed as a hoax. He thought about going outside and checking again what he had seen, and trying to reinterpret it. But something – fear? lethargy? – fixed him here.

And then...

Everything speeded up and he could hardly keep track of things.

The ambulance appeared, closely followed by the police, both arriving in a rumble of engines and rattling of frames over the uneven drive. No sirens.

Tyres skidded to a halt. Engines cut. Doors slammed and there was a murmur of voices and crunch of feet over the gravel that then stopped, followed by the electronic doorbell, the musical trill that Michael had always found twee.

He hurried to the door and nodded as a policeman, middle-aged, ruddy-faced, introduced himself then re-relayed what Michael had said on the phone, the story sounding so absurd. 'Just round the house at the back,' he said, pointing the way. Four burly men plodded along the concrete pathway that he'd swept the snow off last Sunday. Michael pulled on shoes and followed.

The men slowed as they approached the pond; the four of them lined up along one edge and all of them stood – breath clouding the air like bike-shed smokers – and stared. They looked at one another and then at Michael.

'And you've no idea how long this has been here?' the policeman asked, carrying on as if there had been no break in their earlier conversation.

'Not precisely.'

'Or who it is?'

'No.'

The policeman exchanged huddled words with another. He turned towards Michael while his colleague started talking on the phone using words like forensics and back-up.

'Shall we?' the policeman said, touching Michael's arm then gesturing towards the house, as if he were the owner. In front of the house, the ambulance crew was already leaving, probably thinking Michael an idiot, asking for them.

Inside, he found himself offering tea, which the man – what was his name? – said no to; perhaps there was somewhere they could sit and talk, he said. They went into the living room where sinking down into the soft furnishings felt uncomfortable, forcing a lolling position when Michael would have preferred to appear alert.

The man took out a notebook.

The phone rang.

'Probably my wife,' Michael said.

'Go ahead,' the policeman said.

In the hall, he wanted to close the door behind him; but insistence on privacy felt uncomfortable, as if he had something to hide.

'Yes, they're here,' he said to Ciara. 'Just the police now… they're waiting for back-up…I don't know…I don't know…'

He saw how the policeman had come up behind him and was gesturing. 'Hang on,' he told Ciara.

'It would be useful to talk to your wife,' the officer said.

*

Later, after more police had come…

…all of them repeating the same questions, speaking first to him and Ciara separately, and then with Davie small and pale between them and Ciara gently encouraging the child to tell the policeman exactly what he had seen and when…

…and after a whole crowd of uniformed men and women had swarmed around the pond and first there had been endless photographs – the scene brightly lit with halogen lamps cutting through the greyness – and then there had been a complicated procedure involving rotating saws and someone in waders plunging through into the middle of the pond, and Davie had been desperate to see it all from the window until Ciara had abruptly drawn the curtains…

…after Michael had slipped outside, needing air, and had hovered ten yards away as the body shaped object was laid out on a stretcher, as if it might still be alive, and more photos were taken and then the stretcher carried to a white van and strips of red-white barrier tape strung between the trees that crowded round the pond…

…and after a long while of being back inside, suffocating in the overheated air from a crackling fire, when it wasn't clear what else the police could possibly be doing and the three of them were just sitting there in the living room, the TV tuned to a cartoon channel that normally Ciara strictly rationed, unable to move, to do anything…

…after finally someone had come to the door and said they were leaving now and were the family OK and they'd be in touch very soon…

…after it was all over, at least for today, Michael sat there sick with exhaustion and with the horror of the thing.

'Is it still Christmas tomorrow?' Davie asked, his lips as pale as his cheeks.

'Of course it is,' Ciara said. 'Of course.'

*

It was on the local news and then Michael flipped channel and the same story ran at national level. An earnest looking presenter speculated that the girl was the teenager who had gone missing from a children's home a week ago. 'How didn't we know about that?' he asked.

'We did,' Ciara said. 'It was on the local news last week.'

'You didn't say.'

'I don't normally repeat news back to you.'

'I didn't mean that. This morning, you didn't say how it could be her.'

'I didn't think it was. Necessarily. Even now it's only speculation.'

'No, of course. Probably isn't. Probably she just absconded. Headed for London or something,' he said, not knowing why, other than that he didn't want to contemplate the possibility that the face staring back at him from the screen – the teenage girl with peachy skin, self-conscious smile and hair swept up into a ponytail – could have been found dead in his pond.

The TV switched over to a reporter who stood wrapped up against the cold in front of a police barrier and Michael realised with a start that the image was taken at the end of their driveway, that the ghostly barks were their birch trees and the sign on the ramshackle stone wall showed their house-name.

Ciara announced she was going to bed early. Once he might have taken that as a coy suggestion and followed her up; tonight he said he'd be up soon. He was tired but not the kind of tiredness that gives way to sleep. His mind was buzzing and he kept flipping channels, seeking out different news reports, hoping the headlines would be updated and the police be more definite about who the girl was, and how and when and where she'd died, and just why she happened to be in his pond.

The girl had been missing for six days. The fall of snow and the freeze that followed had been three days ago. But he'd been outdoors, making a snowman with Davie at the weekend; he'd have seen if there were bootmarks other than his own and Davie's. Surely.

Nothing added up.

His eyes dragged and he moved from restless wakefulness to a state of such exhaustion that he could not contemplate the effort required to climb the stairs.

*

He woke in a heart-thudding panic, his limbs numb with cold. It took a second for him to realise he was curled up on the sofa. When he moved, his neck creaked painfully. His sleep had been filled with unsettling images. Of blue, translucent figures with featureless faces encased in ice; a mouth opened in a Munch scream; spreading hair and gossamer wings.

He woke again to a solid mass landing across his middle, winding him.

'Davie!' Ciara's said, her voice indulgent.

'It's Christmas, Christmas, Christmas,' Davie said, his fists pummelling Michael's chest.

Michael's neck screeched in pain. He couldn't remember coming to bed or the process of discarding clothes and pulling on pyjamas.

'Hey,' he said and took hold of Davie's wrists and mock-tussled with the squirming, liquid child. His neck hurt and his garden was a crime scene and there might well be reporters camped at the bottom of his drive and it was Christmas.

'He didn't come,' Davie said.

Who?

'I'm sure he did,' Ciara said.

'He didn't, he didn't.' It was impossible to tell if Davie's distress was just the passing mood of a four-year-old or a consequence of yesterday's surreal events.

Ciara was elbowing Michael in the ribs and slowly he realised his failing. It was his job to sneak into Davie's room in the night and fill the oversized Santa sock with the small gifts Ciara had wrapped. His job to take a bite out of the mince pie left out by the blocked off fireplace. All this, while dressed in a hat, beard and outdoor coat, in case his son should happen to wake. All in the aid of furthering an elaborate lie.

Beneath Ciara's smooth smile he felt her annoyance. She could have done it herself or at least issued a reminder. Possibly she wanted to put him in the wrong. Quite likely she had forgotten, given all that had happened, but that didn't stop her blaming him.

'Why don't we go downstairs and I can make you a chocolate shake and then we can go and check together,' Ciara said.

Her body heat withdrew from the duvet and Michael arched his neck back against the pillow before swivelling out of bed to confront the day.

Duties belatedly performed, his tongue washed round his teeth to free them of the cloying sweetness, and his eyes gazed out of the window. Boot marks went every which way across the snow. The red and white of the tape fluttered in the breeze. His heart thumped as he thought he saw movement amidst the bushes.

Just the police. Or a reporter.

Highly unlikely a murderer would return.

He peered harder into the gloom and saw nothing.

*

The three of them gathered in the living room for further presents. Davie was so wired up that whatever he got was bound to be a disappointment. He ripped the paper off the biggest parcel, a tiger cub mauling a rabbit.

'What is it?' he asked, frustrated that the glittery encasing gave way to a garish box and failed to deliver instant gratification. Michael didn't know what it was either. Another year, he and Ciara would have shopped together.

'It's a keyboard,' Ciara explained. 'For making music.' Michael shuddered at the thought of discordant notes filling the thick-walled house.

Ciara helped Davie to break through the layers of cardboard and then plastic bagging, revealing the thing in all its lurid glory.

The phone rang.

'What else is there?' Davie demanded.

Michael got up to take the call.

'Detective Inspector Pollack,' the voice said. 'We have a few more questions.'

'What, now?'

'If that's convenient.'

'It's Christmas Day.'

'I do appreciate that, Sir. But this is a murder investigation.'

He agreed to come to the station. Better that than them disturbing everyone at the house.

'I'll be right back,' he said.

The car was bone-chillingly cold and he had to sit and wait for the engine to get going and the warmth from the heater to demist the windscreen. At the end of the drive he stopped and beeped his horn, then waited for a policeman to get out of his parked car and remove the barrier of tape. The narrow lane was made narrower still by the press vehicles parked up on the grassy verge.

Beyond the house, the lane was empty. Mist hung in the air, reducing visibility so all he could see were his own headlamps carving out beams of lightness, leading the way.

The police station was a concrete municipal building, sitting at the end of a tarmac drive. Doors opened onto a box-like area with thin carpet and magnolia walls and doors heading off every which way. The receptionist was behind glass; a loop of tinsel and several Xmas cards were pinned up on the wall behind her.

Someone would be with him soon.

He sat on the metal bench that was bolted to the floor and read the tacked-up posters. Sixteen people were burgled last year because they didn't lock their own front door.

His hand massaged his stiff neck. He felt the pressure of being made to wait, leaving him uncomfortable and hence more vulnerable, feeling the creep of guilt just by being here.

DI Pollack – the middle-aged, ruddy-faced one – apologised off-handedly as he ushered Michael along echoing corridors and up stairs. Michael wondered whether he cared deeply about the dead girl and the cause of justice being done. Or was he driven by ambition? Did he have a pissed-off wife and disappointed kids at home?

The room was small and windowless; a plywood table was flanked by plastic chairs and had recording equipment at one end. He was introduced to a policewoman, a name he instantly forgot.

'Has the body been identified?' Michael asked.

Pollack looked back at him, his fingers lightly tapping the table, a small smile as if to say we're the ones who ask the questions.

'We've yet to issue a statement.'

Michael was asked to tell his story once again. He heard himself using the exact same words as yesterday and thought something about that sounded suspicious, overly practised. He had practised, the words playing through his mind again and again as he tried to make sense of them.

'Well,' Pollack said, sounding about ready to wind things up and leaving Michael wanting to demand why he'd been called in for an interview that included nothing new. He shifted his chair back a little.

'Just a couple more things…'

Michael froze; he eased his thighs back onto the hard chair.

'If I could just confirm more precisely your movement on the evening of Thursday the 19th of December, between six and midnight.'

The time-slot had been narrowed then. All those men trampling amongst the reeds had derived parameters. A pathologist would have laid the body out and examined it, seeking symptoms, determining a diagnosis.

Cause of death.

Time of.

Length of time submerged beneath the ice.

'I was at home with my wife and son.'

'And was that all evening? From six until midnight?'

It felt like a trick question. 'From…' He cast his mind back, seeking out details that had seemed too unremarkable at the time to note. 'Thursday…' His head nodded in the realisation. 'We had Christmas lunch out. Six of us from the office. A late lunch that carried on all afternoon and afterwards we went home a little early. So I was home by five-thirty. Thereabouts.'

'Had you been drinking?'

'A glass of wine, that's all.' A couple of glasses, perhaps.

'And when you got back, was anyone home?'

'Yes. My wife and son.'

The man's eyes flicked up at him then down at his notebook.

'Actually,' Michael said. It was less than a week ago, but details blurred. 'I was home first, I think it was that night. Davie had something on after school; Ciara was picking him up after and I was the first home.'

'Your wife and son were back when?'

'About six-thirty?' he hazarded. 'Perhaps a little later. I wasn't watching the clock.' He'd crashed out on the bed, regretting the macho-ism of ordering the hottest curry.

'And then…?'

'Ciara would have got on with cooking.' In fact they had argued; she'd demanded to know why he hadn't started cooking given he was home first. 'Then, I don't know, an evening of telly, that kind of thing.' With him and Ciara barely talking to one another, both of them over-jovial with Davie.

'The three of you there all evening?'

'Yes.'

'And your wife will confirm that?'

'Well yes.' Unless… Thursday. It could not be that difficult to remember back. 'Actually Ciara went out. She put Davie to bed and then about eight, eight-thirty, she headed out. Carol rehearsal or something.'

DI Pollack exchanged a quick look with the policewoman.

'That's what she said.'

'And you stayed in the house?'

'Yes. With my son.'

'Who was in bed, asleep?'

'Yes.'

Pollack nodded. 'And there was no one else. No callers? No phone calls.'

'No.'

'And you were doing …what?'

'Still watching telly I guess. Computer gaming perhaps.'

'And you didn't hear or see anything that night?'

'Nothing at all.' It felt like the hundredth time that he had said this. It sounded weak; someone, a man presumably, had brought the girl to the edge of Michael's property. Alive and struggling, or already dead? He had no way to know. The man would've dragged the girl between one of the gaps in the crumbling wall, before crashing through the dead branches that littered the ground. He had dumped the body in the pond, just twenty yards from the house, and Michael hadn't noticed a thing.

'And your wife was back when?'

'I'm not sure. I went to bed.'

'Anything else you remember about the evening? Anything strange?'

'No.'

'Your clothes for example?'

'My clothes?'

Pollack moved abruptly, leaning over the desk. 'Any reason your coat was wet?'

Michael looked into Pollack's impassive eyes. He wanted to demand a lawyer. Absurd, surely. Melodramatic. Suspicious sounding. He'd been viewing too many TV detectives, yarns in which innocent men might be falsely accused. Not that they tended to be convicted, not in the tidy dramas that he favoured as a means of relaxation and which Ciara claimed to despise, though she didn't used to.

'Wet?' The evening appeared all the more blurry the more he thought.

'Something your wife mentioned.'

'She did?' When? Why?

Pollack nodded.

He remembered then, wondering how he hadn't done so instantly. 'I slipped on my way out of the office. The car-park was wet and slippery and I slipped and landed on my backside in a puddle.' Not drunk, but he had been a tiny bit tipsy, just enough to upset his co-ordination a little.

'So your coat was wet when you got home at 5:30?'

'Yes.'

'But you didn't do anything to dry it off or bring it to your wife's attention?'

'No.'

'And you weren't drunk?'

'No!' Denying it so vigorously instantly felt like a mistake.

'OK, Mr Collins.' Pollack sat back in his chair. 'I wondered if you would mind giving a DNA sample. Just a saliva swab. Eliminating possibilities.' The man's smile was as icy as the pond.

*

Back home, he was greeted by the electronic screech of Davie's new toy. Whatever had possessed Ciara? Within the dissonance, he detected a couple of bars from Silent Night. The house stank of singed animal fat and overcooked sprouts.

He waited for Ciara to come into the hallway to greet him. She didn't; she barely looked up as he entered the living room.

'Sorry,' he said, though why the hell he was apologising, he didn't know. 'It took longer than I'd expected.'

She nodded.

'Have you both eaten?'

'Well yes. I had no idea when you'd be back and everything was ready.'

'Right. Well I'll just...' He gestured the kitchen. Davie banged the keyboard with force. 'Is there not a volume control on that?'

Ciara didn't deign to answer.

'And why the fuck did you tell the police my coat was all wet last Thursday?'

It was rare that he swore in front of Davie; the boy continued his vigorous assault on the keyboard. Ciara looked back coolly. 'Why wouldn't I answer their questions honestly?' And there was something in her face, some look he couldn't fathom, and the more he looked the less he seemed to see.

'Just when did you get back that night?'

'I was with someone. I'm fully vouched for.'

It was a strange answer. Only when he was in the kitchen, retrieving from the oven a plate of meat and vegetables under congealed gravy, did he think that.

What did she mean: fully vouched for?

*

The following days passed minute by minute. Outside remained subsumed in mist and they stayed indoors, letting Davie spend too long with his computer games, too long watching telly, the frenetic onscreen activities a rebuke for the real-life lack of exercise that left the boy fractious and whiney. Michael and Ciara avoided being alone together.

The phone rang over and over and each time Michael's heart rocketed to his throat. Sometimes it was yet another friend or relative wishing them Merry Christmas and wanting to hear the details. Sometimes it was a reporter offering money for the inside story. *And how has it affected you as a family?*

Michael and Ciara watched the news and endless reporters repeated the same facts, filling the screen with that same photo. Jeannette, the girl was called. Just sixteen. Had been in care since she was three. A lovely girl, various people said, very bright, well liked, as if her death would matter less if she hadn't been those things. After TV reports failed to turn up anything new, Michael switched to Google, discovering so-called details on the gossip sites. It was said she slept around. That she did drugs. That she favoured older men who gave her money. Staring at the screen, she appeared more and more familiar. Might he have passed her in the street or supermarket? Or perhaps one night, she'd occupied a corner of the bar while he downed a couple of pints with colleagues and he caught her smile, half-seductive, and just for a second he'd been tempted. He could almost see it in his mind's eye. He was about to search more deeply, to click on another link, when it came to him how online activity could be tracked and his curiosity might seem obsessive.

It was early evening two days after Boxing Day when the electronic tinkle of the doorbell interrupted Michael amidst suds and greasy dishes.

'I'll get it,' Michael called out as he dried his hands. The uniformed officer was not one he recognised.

Behind Michael, Ciara was attempting to usher Davie upstairs, but the boy clung fiercely to her leg.

'We'll be issuing a press release very shortly,' the policeman said. 'We thought we should let you know first.'

A man had been arrested and was being held for questioning. A boyfriend apparently. Or rather ex-boyfriend; it was thought Jeanette had planned to end the relationship.

Later that evening Michael and Ciara heard it on the news. The man – just a teenager – looked so young, his face scattered with acne, his eyes cast-down. Michael turned the TV off and he and Ciara sat in silence. For a moment their stillness felt almost companionable and he thought how he might reach for her hand and search for something tender to say. But edge of vision something nagged, causing him to tighten, then to speak.

'Who were you with that evening?' he asked.

He waited for her to trot out pat explanations involving some old lady from the church. He heard the intake of her breath. 'He's called Chris,' she said.

*

Events moved forward with slow inevitability. Later, looking back, he was almost surprised to discover months had passed, not just a week or two.

He and Ciara tried to talk, but what was there to say, I mean really. She'd been seeing Chris – fucking him, to be precise – for six months. They'd met at church. Six months and Michael had not noticed anything, not really, and that apparently was the problem. He didn't see her; she'd changed and he hadn't noticed.

And what about Christian morals, didn't they preclude shagging someone else's wife? Being unfaithful to your husband? It felt too hypocritical to ask.

Pollack came round to deliver the details he thought they were owed, his ruddy face revealing no trace of apology. The girl had been strangled. Not in their garden; she'd probably been dead for a day or so before entering the water. Initially the body must have been weighted down amongst the reeds, but it had been done ineptly. The water began to freeze. The body worked loose from its anchorage and rose until it lay there, trapped behind the layer of ice. Forensic evidence suggested she'd put up a spirited fight.

Perhaps Michael might have fought harder for his marriage. Perhaps he might have found better means of persuasion, better arguments for trying again. But what haunted him wasn't so much the thought of Ciara's freckled flesh in another man's bed, but the memory of her look. The look which said that his innocence was not being taken entirely for granted, that questions were being asked and all sorts of possibilities being considered.

*

The house felt permanently cold now it was just Michael living there. The air felt tainted.

He sat with the TV on and stared at the armchair where Ciara used to curl up, slippered feet tucked behind, while images of the girl – splayed beneath the ice – replayed in his mind. He drained his glass of whisky and poured another.

The phone rang. He badly didn't want to talk to anyone, but neither could he bear the depth of silence that random blaring from the TV failed to disperse. Standing up too quickly, he reached out a hand to steady himself. Not drunk. Just a little tipsy.

'Yeah,' he said into the phone.

'It's me.' Ciara.

'So it is.' But sarcasm had always been lost on Ciara.

'About the weekend. I don't think Davie should sleep over at the house.'

He paused, his hand fisting round the phone, trying to master himself. 'We agreed.'

'I know we agreed and this isn't about me, it's about Davie. He doesn't like sleeping there.'

'He was fine last time.' The boy had woken with nightmares, but bad dreams were hardly unusual for a four-year-old.

'He was not fine! He was terrified. When he came home he did nothing but talk about ghosts coming to get him and he didn't sleep for the next two nights.'

'You're turning him against me.'

'Nonsense. I'm trying to do what's in his interest.'

'You and Chris.'

'Chris is very fond of Davie and we both want what's best for him.'

He thought of Chris – a guitar-strumming Cliff Richard type from what he'd seen – playing father to his son. Putting him to bed. Reading stories, probably from the frigging bible. Playing wholesome board games, because he didn't believe electronic games were good for a child. Helping out at bath time and feeling the boy's slippery sealskin beneath his hands.

'The two of you have got him babbling about Jesus and Holy Ghosts and god knows what. No wonder he's started being frightened of supernatural things with all that crap being thrown at him.'

The pause lingered. He was damned if he was going to break it.

'He's my son too.' Ciara's voice was measured and controlled. 'Chris and I are both very involved in the church. I'm not forcing Davie. He seems to find the idea of God and heaven comforting, and after all he's been through, I'm not taking that away. Like you've always said, he'll make up his own mind when he's an adult.'

Michael's hand tightened further and he didn't trust himself to speak as he carried on strangling the phone.

'It will be different when you've found somewhere else to live,' Ciara continued, her voice the epitome of reasonableness.

Bitch! She knew very well that the mortgage and maintenance payments were crippling him financially and that with events so fresh no one was likely to touch the house.

He had nightmares too.

Much later, he woke in the middle of the night, sweat-drenched with panic, the fragments of his dream already slipping away. He sprang out of bed and stood at the window, looking down into the garden that was lit under a full moon. And then, without quite knowing why, he found himself fleeing from the room and stumbling – his mind sleep and alcohol befuddled – down the stairs and through the kitchen and outdoors, heading towards the pond which glimmered in the white light. He shivered violently.

And then he felt it. Something. He couldn't say what.

The Angel

*

Saturday was dreary. Michael granted Ciara no more than a nod as she stood in the doorway of the redbrick terraced house, her smile fake, her hands resting on Davie's shoulders. Davie was bundled up in that colourful scarf and looked uncertainly from his mother to his father. Michael crouched down to be level with him and tousled his hair, which only recently had ceased being baby-soft. 'I hear you don't want to sleep over,' he said.

Davie shook his head.

'OK. Not this time. Not if you don't want to.'

'Or even go to the house,' Ciara said.

Michael shot her a look of pure hatred.

A whole day was going to be difficult to fill, especially when the weather was so dismal and they'd already seen the latest cartoon at the cinema several times.

'And no swimming. Not today,' Ciara added. 'He has a bit of a cold.'

They went to the park to look at the ducks but the sight of the park lake set Davie's fingernails biting into Michael's palms. They headed to the play-area with its swings and rain-splattered slide.

The steady drizzle turned heavier. It was only eleven o'clock. 'McDonalds for lunch?' Michael asked. 'That might be fun.'

Davie nodded anxiously.

They chose a booth by the window, settling into the arse-shaped seats that would become uncomfortable after about five minutes. At the table next to them someone was reading one of the tabloids whose inner page featured the face that haunted him, the girl with self-conscious smile and ponytail.

The body had been buried yesterday.

It was too late to distract Davie from seeing it; he stared and stared and forgot his burger that dripped orange grease down his sleeve.

'Is she an angel now?' Davie asked.

No, Michael wanted to say. The girl was nothing now. All of them turned to nothing in the end, to lumps of flesh left to rot or be incinerated. But that didn't mean you had to live your life that way, as if it were nothing. He wanted his son to understand this. It was life's transience – the absoluteness of its end – that somehow made it bearable.

But there was no way of explaining any of that, not to a four-year-old.

No. It came back to him then, that strange nighttime sense of something warm sparking through him, the sense he had had of another presence. He couldn't explain that either. He placed his hand over his son's and wished he could pass on to Davie the deep peacefulness he had felt, standing, frozen through yet warm, at the edges of the pond.

'Yes,' he said. 'I'm sure she must be. An angel.'

LITTLE THINGS

RUBY COWLING

That four-second shot of Zanimation's new feature The Gerbil Princess showed Scruttle, the cockroach servant, extending two of his six limbs and pushing open the banqueting room's golden double doors, revealing an exquisitely laden oak table. That was all. Bob wanted it super-smooth, meaning twenty-four separate frames per second. Bob wanted a lot.

Bob said, Doug, we've got to take the long hours if we're going to kick Pixar's ass.

I thought, we say arse.

Once Golden Boy upstairs had done the keys, it was up to us basement ants to do the donkeywork: the tweening. So for the last three weeks I'd been hairlining Scruttle's little arms and legs with a black-dabbed 6/0 brush; yellowing-in the eighteen perfect brass buttons on his uniform; lightening every shade in tiny increments as those doors gradually – so gradually – came open.

On Saturday, Laurie brought my 7am tea and Nurofen as usual, but she wasn't happy I was going in at the weekend.

What can I do, sweets? Bob said Monday, latest, and there's only me and Adora-the-intern left downstairs since DreamFeedR pulled funding.

Adora, snorted Laurie from the bathroom, you've got to be kidding.

She's Spanish, I whispered.

Little Things

*

Adora was head-down, opposite me, sharing the lamp-lit quiet of the Saturday office. The soft tips of her hair caressing the acetate. I pencilled Scruttle's stupid tasselled epaulettes for the twentieth time, holding my breath until sparks pinged through my vision. At six, Adora got up and stretched, baring the tiny shell of her navel.

Hometime! she said, and swung out. I was lightheaded.

Laurie was curled on the sofa watching the lottery draw, didn't hear my honey, I'm home. She loved that corny stuff when we first moved in to this little place, corridoring through boxes, wearing each other like backpacks. Now the flat seemed oddly spacious. Maybe it was my microcosmic work squint, magnifying the gaps between things in the real world. But wait – there really were fewer coats in the hall.

Having a clear-out, Laur?

Mmm, she said.

*

Sunday, late afternoon. If we'd had a window, we'd have been humbled by an immense sunset. But we didn't. Across from Adora in her pool of golden light I retouched the candleshine curves of four thousand heaped banquet grapes, until actual tears brimmed and rolled.

Fancy a drink? I blurted. That Wetherspoon's's got an offer on?

A drink? Adora laughed, not looking up. With you?

I went home to my Laurie.

She had finished clearing out.

For the next fortnight, at noon each day, I got a single text:

Just

A

Little

Bit

Of

Attention

To

Detail
Each
Day
Would
Have
Been
Nice.

UNTHOLOGISTS

Rodge Glass is the author of six books: the novels No Fireworks (Faber, 2005), Hope for Newborns (Faber, 2008) and Bring Me the Head of Ryan Giggs (Tindal Street Press, 2012), also a graphic novel, Dougie's War (Freight Books, 2010), a literary biography, Alasdair Gray: A Secretary's Biography (Bloomsbury, 2008) and most recently LoveSexTravelMusik (Freight, 2013), a collection of travel short stories. His work has won a Somerset Maugham award and been nominated for numerous other prizes. He regularly appears on BBC Radio and is a Senior Lecturer in Creative Writing at Edge Hill University.

Carys Bray's short story collection Sweet Home is published by Salt. Carys lives in Southport with her husband and four children and she has just finished writing her first novel.

Michael Crossan was a Glimmer Train Top 25 Open Fiction Finalist, December 2012. He was shortlisted for the Bridport Short Story Prize and The Scottish Book Trust New Writers Award in 2011. His short stories have been published in online literary journals. His novel – Eden Dust – is written. Michael's blog is michaelcwrites.wordpress.com, and his Twitter account is @michaelcrossann.

Sarah Bower is a prize-winning short story writer and the author of two critically acclaimed historical novels, The Needle in the Blood (Susan Hill's Novel of the Year 2007) and The Book of Love (published in the US as Sins of the House of Borgia) Her work has been translated into nine languages. Sins of the House of Borgia was an international bestseller. Her third novel, Erosion, is scheduled for publication in 2013. She is currently working on a short story commission for BBC Radio 4. Sarah lives in Suffolk and will be writer in residence at Lingnan University, Hong Kong in 2014.

Barnaby Walsh was born and lives in Lancashire. He recently completed his MA in creative writing at the University of Manchester, and was joint runner-up in this year's Willesden Herald international short story competition.

Rowena Macdonald was born on the Isle of Wight in 1974, grew up in the West Midlands and now lives in east London. Smoked Meat, her debut collection of short stories, was published by Flambard Press in 2011. In 2012 it was shortlisted for the Edge Hill Prize and longlisted for the Frank O'Connor Prize. Rowena works as a secretary at the House of Commons and teaches creative writing at Westminster University.

Adrian Slatcher was born in Staffordshire, and has lived in Manchester for the last 20 years. He has published poetry and short stories and also writes music. He regularly blogs about literature at www.artoffiction.blogspot.com. His poetry has recently appeared in the Rialto, Sculpted: Poets of the NW and Catechism: Poems for Pussy Riot. The story The Cat came to him in a dream.

Melanie Whipman grew up in Brighton, and has lived in Germany, France and Israel. She has now settled in a Surrey village with her husband, teenage twins, dog, cats and chickens. She has an MA in Creative Writing for which she won the Kate Betts Prize and is currently a PhD student. Her short stories have been published in various magazines and anthologies and broadcast on Radio 4, and her novel-in-progress was long-listed for the Cinnamon Press First Novel Award. When she's not writing she teaches creative writing in Farnham.

Joshua Allen was born twenty-five years ago in Kent. At the age of fourteen, he discovered that his biological father was the Azerbaijani poet Avraamy Naghiyev, who perished in the Batken mining disaster. Joshua graduated with a first class BA in English Literature and Philosophy from the University of East Anglia. Subsequently, he completed UEA's Creative Writing MA. His prose has appeared in Unthology 2 and UEA Creative Writing Anthology 2012. He currently teaches and writes in Istanbul.

Marc Owen Jones lives in Norwich with his wife and two daughters. He's a company director and writes to relax. He has previously written a musical and two short films. This is his first short story.

Aiden O'Reilly completed a masters degree in mathematics and published papers on a quantum mechanical dynamical system. After a crisis of faith in science, he abandoned his PhD studies and lived in Germany and Eastern Europe for several years. He has worked variously as a translator, building-site worker, property magazine editor, and IT teacher. In November 2008 he won the McLaverty Award, awarded biannually for short stories. He received an Arts Council bursary in 2012. His collection of short stories has been accepted for publication by Honest Publishing. www.aidenoreilly.com

Sarah Evans has had dozens of stories published in magazines and competition anthologies. Recently, her story 'Shadower' won the Bloomsbury crime-story competition and 'Blue Flowers' appeared in the 2013 Rubery Press anthology. She has been an Unthologist twice previously and other stories have been published by Bridport, Earlyworks Press, Bridge House, Writers' Forum, Sentinel Champions Magazine and many more. She lives in Welwyn Garden City with her husband and non-writing interests include walking and opera.

Ruby Cowling grew up in West Yorkshire and lives in London. Winner of the Words With Jam Short Story Competition 2012 (judged by Jane Fallon), Highly Commended in the Bridport Prize 2012 (judged by Patrick Gale), and a Micro Award 2013 nominee, her short fiction has appeared in various literary magazines and anthologies; most recently at Punchnel's, The View From Here and (in audio format) 4'33". She is currently working on a short story collection.

Lightning Source UK Ltd.
Milton Keynes UK
UKOW04f0032051113

220438UK00006B/719/P